Saltwater Crossing

Press

Pittsburgh

This is a work of fiction. Names, characters, businesses, places, events, locales, and incidents are either the products of the author's imagination or used in a fictitious manner. Any resemblance to actual persons, living or dead, or actual events is purely coincidental.

While every precaution has been taken in the preparation of this book, the publisher assumes no responsibility for errors or omissions, or for damages resulting from the use of the information contained herein.

SALTWATER CROSSING

ANJ Press, First edition. December 2020.

Copyright © 2020 Amelia Addler.

Written by Amelia Addler.

Cover design by Charmaine Ross at CharmaineRoss.com

Maps by Nate Taylor at IllustratorNate.com

For the moments that make us stop and change course

Recap and Introduction to *Saltwater Crossing*

Welcome to the fourth book in the Westcott Bay Series! In book one, our heroine Margie Clifton moved to San Juan Island following her divorce to start her event hosting business at Saltwater Cove. She also hoped to make a second home for her three kids Tiffany, Jade and Connor.

Margie's life was turned upside down when she discovered that her ex-husband Jeff spent decades hiding a secret child, Morgan Allen, from an affair with the late Kelly Allen. With the help of Chief Hank, Margie was able to piece her life back together and reunite her family – including the new addition of Morgan.

In book two of the series, Morgan moved to San Juan Island and fell in love with Luke Pierce, a charming yet infuriating Brit. Luke's uncle just happened to be Brock Hunter – a man suspected of being involved in the hit-and-run death of her mom Kelly. With Luke's help, Morgan discovers that Brock's girlfriend Andrea was actually behind the wheel of the 1963 Corvette Stingray that hit her mother.

Andrea is arrested and awaiting trial in book three, while Jade faces her new life after her divorce from Brandon. She throws herself into a community project to decide what to do with a plot of land left to San Juan County by former resident Colby Smith. Her dedication is a threat to powerful island residents, though, and her home is burned down in retaliation.

Luckily, Matthew is there to rescue her, leaving Jade free to catch the ill-meaning council member Jared Knape in the plot that threatened her life.

In book four, Jade leads the committee overseeing the project on Colby's land. She's happy to work with Eric and Sidney Burke, who were formerly her competition, in building a new park on Colby's land. Meanwhile, Morgan is preoccupied with Andrea's trial for her mom's hit-and-run. Tiffany, whose world was shaken after her friend Malcolm died of cancer, leaves her high-powered finance job in Chicago and moves in with Jade to help her build the new state park. Tiffany's newest challenge has nothing to do with permits or council members, but instead a pair of dark brown eyes belonging to the ever-scowling Sidney Burke...

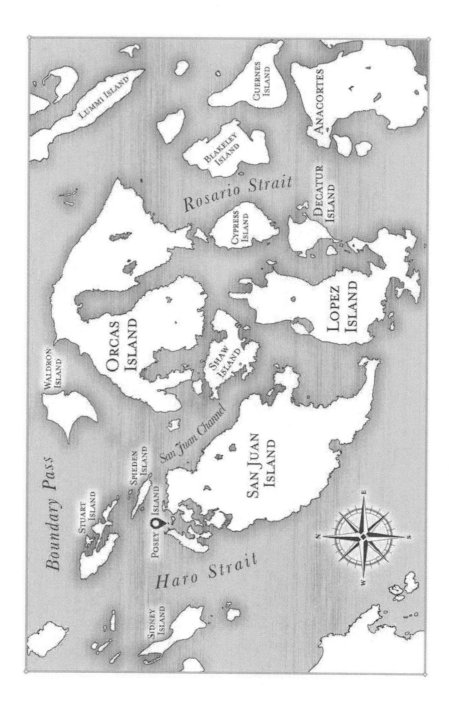

POSEY ISLAND

San Juan Channel

Westcott Bay

Saltwater Cove

SAN JUAN ISLAND

Friday Harbor

Cattle Point

Lime Kiln

Haro Strait

N E S W

Chapter 1

If she stood back far enough, the ballroom *almost* looked like one of her old work events. Tiffany smiled. It seemed that people ignored the "optional" in the "black tie optional" dress code; the women were either in cocktail dresses or floor-length gowns, and most of the men were in tuxedos.

Who knew that the Milky Way Star Awards would be the social event of the season?

"Oh, there's one," Tiffany said under her breath.

Jade looked over to her. " 'There's one' what?"

Tiffany subtly pointed out a man who was across the room. "A guy that showed up in khakis."

Jade laughed. "Why does that matter?"

"It's actually better than I expected," Tiffany said, finishing off a glass of champagne and setting it on a nearby table. "I thought that half of the people here would be dressed like Steve Irwin."

"What's wrong with Steve Irwin? I loved – no – I *still* love him. He was an inspiration and – "

Tiffany waved a hand. "Oh stop, we *all* loved him. I just didn't think that a group of park rangers and forest lumberjacks would get so...dressed up."

"Ah I see," said Jade. "Though I don't think anyone here is a lumberjack."

"You know what I mean."

Jade smiled. "C'mon Tiffany! This is a *national* awards program! It's a big deal. Parks and recreation *professionals* from all across the country gathered to celebrate and – "

Tiffany laughed, cutting her off. "All right, all right! I'm just surprised that these *professionals* didn't wear their khaki outfits and ranger hats. Maybe a little disappointed, if I'm honest."

"I've been thinking about getting a ranger hat..." Jade said dreamily.

"I can see that. That would work for you."

"Oh my gosh!" Jade dropped her voice to a whisper. "That's the director of Oregon State Parks. Do you think I could say hello? She looks busy."

Tiffany looked over. "She doesn't look busy. Go for it. I'll stay here and guard this corner."

She watched as her sister slowly and cautiously made her way to the small group of "parks and recreation professionals." After she was satisfied that Jade had been welcomed into the group, Tiffany peered at the bar to see how long the line was. It looked like it would take forever. Maybe if she stood around long enough someone would bring her something.

She heard her phone go off and dug it out of her purse to have a look – it was her old neighbor wishing her a happy birthday.

Ugh.

She wrote back a thank you and tucked her phone away, making sure to silence it this time. This certainly wasn't how she had imagined spending her 30th birthday – but this wasn't where she thought she'd *be* at age thirty, either.

She was unemployed, living off of her savings, while sharing a rental house with her sisters Jade and Morgan. And despite everything she'd done in her life to that point – the advanced classes, her 3.9 GPA in college, the stack of credits for an MBA – none of it mattered.

She'd done everything right. So how did she end up so lost?

A guy having an animated conversation bumped into her.

"Oh I'm so sorry ma'am," he said before walking away.

Ma'am!

That was *quite* enough. She didn't care how long the line was for the bar – she wasn't going to stand around like the old spinster that she was and be called *ma'am!*

Tiffany walked over and took a spot at the end of the line for the bar. Everyone around her was engaged in pleasant conversations. She bit her lip – maybe she should try to talk to someone? But what about?

She wasn't used to going to events like this and not knowing anyone; and she definitely wasn't used to feeling out of place. With her old job, she knew exactly what she was doing and what her purpose was. She knew people, too – who to schmooze and who to listen to, who to avoid.

She'd known, then, what she wanted. Or at least she thought she did.

Tiffany stood for a few minutes, watching the people around her, until she gave up on her idea of making friends and pulled her phone out – it was best to look somewhat busy.

Her new thing was trying to resist looking at her phone so often; one of the many self-improvement books that she'd read recommended turning it off for a few hours a day.

She wasn't *quite* there yet – especially when she was stuck in an awkward situation like this. The book said that by using her phone to avoid feeling uncomfortable, she was only avoiding her feelings and that she'd have to deal with them eventually.

The book was a little extreme, in her opinion.

What if someone needed to reach her? Not that she knew who that would be, exactly – she was home most of the time and no one needed her to do anything anymore. Even her old coworkers seemed to forget that she existed.

Some of her friends stayed in touch, sure. But after quitting her job, a job that took up almost all of her time, she realized how empty her life was. And that feeling, that realization, only made her want to reach for her phone even more.

Her head was down, scrolling through Instagram posts of people looking happy when she thought she heard someone say San Juan Island.

She looked up, trying to pinpoint where she'd heard it. It didn't take long – about ten feet ahead of her in line were two people that she actually *did* recognize – Eric and Sidney Burke.

Tiffany was able to mostly hide behind the group in front of her as she studied them. They were both impeccably dressed in custom-fitted tuxedos.

No surprise there. They came from a wealthy family, and Eric especially had qualities that screamed "growing up with money."

Not that Tiffany disliked him, or anything. It was just something she'd noticed about him over the past few weeks. He'd spent so much time heavily campaigning for Jade's and the committee's attention for the bid to build on Colby's land – it was impossible to miss him.

Tiffany found Eric interesting. Even though he had lost the vote to Jade on what to build on the land, he still really wanted to be involved with the project. He seemed so genuinely *excited* about it. Jade was excited too, so the two of them talked and sent ideas back and forth day after day.

Tiffany wasn't *that* crazy about the project – she just wanted to help Jade. But it was odd to watch Jade and Eric's mutual thrill build off one another; and Eric didn't know this yet, but his company had a very good shot at being the one chosen to build the park.

Actually, they had the *only* shot. Eric had, completely unprompted, gotten architects and engineers to design 3D models and virtual tours of his plans for the park. He brought samples of materials to the committee. No other company came close to his enthusiasm or to the thoroughness of his plans.

Tiffany wondered how much it was costing him, but she couldn't ask.

Yet.

Jade loved all of the ideas, and even when she had questions, Eric was flexible, adjusting the models with her suggestions. The committee was quite smitten with Burke Development.

It seemed a sure thing, really. Tiffany didn't care, as long as it worked for the budget. They were actually at the Milky Way Awards because Jade was accepting a grant to turn Colby's land into a Washington State Park.

She'd written the grant proposal almost entirely on her own – though admittedly, Eric did help with that a bit as well. At least the man seemed to know what he wanted.

But why was he so intent on building on San Juan Island? Tiffany had no idea. She stood there, not meaning to eavesdrop, but she couldn't avoid it unless she walked away. And she couldn't lose her place in line – not now when she was so close.

"Oh you have *got* to see it, it's just a beautiful place," Eric said.

Tiffany leaned forward slightly, trying to make it look like she was focused on her phone as she strained to listen.

"Yeah...sounds cool," said an unfamiliar voice.

Tiffany stole a glance to see that it was a woman who'd spoken, wrapped in a skin-tight cocktail dress, her back almost entirely exposed. Tiffany was surprised that she hadn't noticed her before when she was looking at everyone's outfits – it was the most risqué dress in the ballroom. The fabric looked almost painted on.

She didn't look like a park ranger – she was definitely someone's date. So either whoever brought her didn't tell her how formal the event was, or she was too young to know better.

And she did look young. Twenty, *maybe?* Tiffany knew that Eric was married; his wife had even come to San Juan Island once to meet everyone and see the sites. So perhaps this girl was Sidney's date?

"Gross," Tiffany muttered to herself.

She'd forgotten about Sidney; he didn't come around nearly as often as Eric did. Apparently he was busy cruising college campuses for girls almost half his age to be impressed by his expensive suits and self-important attitude.

"Yeah, we'll see what happens," Sidney said, letting out a sigh.

"Oh come on," replied Eric, smiling broadly. "You've been dancing around this for weeks. What do you want to say about the park? Come on, I can take it."

Sidney shook his head. "No, I'm not dancing around anything. There's nothing to say until we hear if we've won the bid."

"Come on Sid, where's your sense of adventure? I've been working with Jade almost every day. And she's full of ideas and just a lovely, charming person."

Tiffany couldn't help but smile. Eric was right – Jade *was* a lovely person. Anyone who was good to Jade was good in her book. His puppy-like enthusiasm was really growing on her.

"You can't wait around for her business forever just because she's nice."

"I know, but she's the head of the committee," replied Eric. "And she likes our ideas."

"I'm not worried about the committee," said Sidney. "They don't seem to have much power at all. It's her bodyguard that scares me."

Okay, now Tiffany knew that she shouldn't be listening, but she couldn't help it. She turned her back to them so they wouldn't see her, but made sure to turn her good ear in their direction.

"She has a bodyguard?" the girl asked, her interest finally piqued.

"What, do you mean her boyfriend, the cop?" asked Eric. "He's harmless. Matthew's a really nice guy, actually."

"No, not him." Sidney put in an order for a club soda. "Her sister. The stone-faced one."

Eric laughed. "What do you mean?"

"I know women like her. It doesn't matter how nice Jade is, because her sister is always there, in her power suit, thinking she's cleverer than everyone. She's the one you have to worry about."

Tiffany raised her eyes from her phone and slowly turned, unable to control her glare.

None of them saw her; they were all focused on accepting their drinks from the bartender. She continued staring at Sidney as the three of them walked by. Their conversation never broke and no one noticed her. It was like she didn't exist.

Well then.

Thirty didn't seem like it was off to a good start.

Tiffany put her phone back into her purse just as Jade appeared behind her.

"Hey, there you are! I'm sorry that took so long – we got into a really interesting conversation about crushed limestone for hiking paths."

"Oh, it's okay," Tiffany said, mind still swimming with what she'd heard.

Jade frowned. "I'm *really* sorry! Don't be mad at me – I won't leave you again."

Tiffany shook her head and forced herself to smile. "No, really, it's fine! I'm glad you found someone to talk to about limestone hiking paths. I've just been waiting in this line for a while."

"Oh okay. Well I think that we should get our drinks and then head to our seats, we don't want to miss the keynote speaker."

Tiffany had to resist teasing Jade; it was the third time she'd mentioned that she didn't want to be late for this speaker. "Sure. That sounds like a plan."

"Okay. Wait – I think I just saw Eric! He's one of the sponsors – I saw a table with a Burke Development sign on it. We should stop by and say hello before we take our seats."

Tiffany smiled. Now *that* could be entertaining. "What a great idea."

Chapter 2

They made their way back to their sponsor table. Sidney took a sip of his club soda as Eric stumbled over a bit of carpet; he threw out an arm to steady him.

Good thing Sidney was the one driving tonight.

"I hope we didn't miss anyone while we were gone," said Eric once he recovered from his misstep.

"I wouldn't worry about that," Sidney replied.

Hardly anyone had come to talk to them and they'd been standing at that table for almost two hours. Maybe people would stop by later? But it seemed unlikely.

"When do we get to sit down?" asked Rachel. "My shoes are killing me."

"Soon! We don't want to miss any potential customers," Eric said, smiling broadly. "It's so important that the new business gets as much exposure as it can, especially since I want to get into doing more parks – this is the perfect place to meet people."

Rachel crossed her arms and said nothing.

Sidney frowned. He'd started bringing her to more work events and meetings in order to expose her to the real world – and the family business.

So far, everything he'd shown her failed to capture her attention. She looked bored and she didn't ask questions or follow conversations. Worse, she hardly managed to keep off of her phone when one of the partners talked to her last week. He thought that was incredibly rude and had to have a serious talk with her.

And now she was hanging off of the table and pouting. It was actually her idea to come to this event, so he didn't know what changed. He was excited that she'd shown some initiative. Perhaps it ended up being less glamorous than she'd expected?

"Hello hello!" said a familiar voice.

Sidney looked up to see Jade and her sister.

"Just the person I was hoping to see!" said Eric, walking around the table to give her a hug.

Sidney never got behind the whole hugging people thing. It weirded him out. What if someone took it the wrong way? He wasn't a hugging sort of person; luckily people seemed to enjoy hugging Eric and left him out of it.

Sidney offered a handshake to them both, which they accepted.

"I love what you've got set up here," Jade said, studying the models and boards.

"Thank you! This was my first time putting all of this together. With Sidney's help, of course."

Sidney nodded.

"It looks great," said the sister.

"I'm so sorry – do you remember my cousin Sidney?" Eric motioned to his left. "And this is his sister, Rachel."

Rachel smiled and waved.

"It's nice to meet you Rachel. I'm Jade and this is *my* sister Tiffany."

"Ah, are you getting into the family business, Rachel?" asked Tiffany.

Rachel shrugged. "I guess so."

"I'm sure Rachel will find her niche – if that's what she wants to do! Though it did take me almost ten years to figure out what I wanted to be doing," said Eric with a laugh. "Who knew it would be parks and recreation!"

Sidney resisted saying anything. True, this was the first time that Eric's dad was allowing him to take such drastic direction with Burke Development – but Eric had had plenty of ill-fated ideas before.

If this didn't work out, though, it would be his worst failure yet. Somehow, Sidney needed to make sure that didn't happen.

"I don't know about you guys, but I am *so* excited for this," Jade continued. "Did you look at the program? There are all kinds of awards – excellence in rangering, trail innovation, environmental achievement..."

"And your very impressive grant!" added Eric.

"Yes." Jade smiled. "Can't forget that. Well, we're going to run to our seats. But maybe we can catch up later?"

"That would be nice," said Eric. "Enjoy!"

Eric was still beaming when another group approached the table. Sidney decided to excuse himself for a moment – he'd rejoin them once the award ceremony started. He needed to make a few work phone calls that he'd been putting off.

Sidney found a comfortable spot that was quiet enough for him to make the calls. He made the mistake of looking at his email – there were a few that he needed to respond to right away. He answered those and the calls took longer than he expected; he ended up missing the first hour of speakers and awards.

Once he fumbled his way to his seat in the dark, he settled in and was happy to see that he'd made it in time to watch Jade accept her award. Perhaps now that it was official, she could make a decision about who would be building the park on San Juan Island.

Though Eric had boundless energy and ideas for this project, Sidney thought it was imprudent to keep spending time and money on something that didn't have a guaranteed return. His uncle made it clear that Eric only had a year to get his idea off the ground or he would be killing that branch of the company.

He tasked Sidney with "helping" Eric – basically a babysitting job. And Eric had already used a few months on this project, thinking it'd be the star in his portfolio.

Sidney shifted in his seat and looked at Eric. He was enthralled by the awards, a look of glee on his face. It would be tough to convince him to move on if this project didn't pan out.

After a few minutes, Sidney realized that Rachel was missing.

He leaned over to Eric and whispered, "Where's Rachel?"

"I think she went to the bathroom," Eric replied, eyes still focused on the stage.

Sidney looked at the program. It seemed that the ceremony was about to come to an end, and Rachel was nowhere to be seen.

He had a sinking feeling that something wasn't quite right. He pulled out his cell phone and opened up an app that tracked all of the phones on his plan.

Among other things, Sidney paid for Rachel's cell phone. Their father was unwilling or unable to pay for much these days, so Sidney was Rachel's only option. And Rachel's mother, Sidney's step-mother, had gotten used to a standard of living that was quickly evaporating with his father's worsening alcoholism.

The app loaded and he watched as the little symbol for Rachel made its way down the freeway, headed right into Seattle.

He nudged Eric, showing him the screen. "It looks like we've lost Rachel."

"I'm sorry," he whispered. "I got so distracted – I didn't think she was going to pull a runner."

"It's fine. As soon as this is done we can go and find out what she's up to."

Sidney felt a tightening in his throat. What *was* she up to? It seemed like she'd planned to wait until Sidney wasn't paying attention.

But what if something had happened to her? She was only eighteen – and it seemed that Rachel was at the stage where she had enough energy to execute all of her ideas without the experience to identify which of them were ill-advised.

What had she gotten into her head now? She'd already had a tough year at school, getting in trouble for skipping class and driving irresponsibly with her friends.

She'd rear-ended someone at a stop sign, and Sidney made the decision to take her car away – the police told him that she'd been texting!

That didn't win many points for him, but he didn't care. She needed to learn to be responsible, and it became clear to him that no one else was willing to make the hard decisions like that. Also, he'd bought her the car – and paid for her insurance. He couldn't let her walk all over him.

Thankfully, the ceremony ended and everyone got up and started chatting. Sidney was halfway to the door when he turned around to find that Eric hadn't made it very far – he was talking to Tiffany and Jade.

He sighed. It was going to be difficult to tear him away – or maybe he should just leave him behind?

No – two heads were better than one. He looked at his phone and saw that Rachel had stopped moving. He Googled the address and saw that it was for a nightclub called Heaven.

Terrific.

"Hey Eric, we've got to head out," he said. "Unless you want to stay – "

"No, I think you're going to need backup."

Jade's eyes darted between them. "Is everything okay?"

"It seems that my little cousin pulled a fast one on us," said Eric with a laugh. "You know, she's at that age – she gets ideas."

When Eric put it like that, it seemed like harmless fun – but it wasn't. She could get herself into serious trouble, and they were supposed to be responsible for her. How had they let her disappear like this?

Sidney cleared his throat. "It looks like she's gotten into some sort of a nightclub. I have no idea how – she's only eighteen. She shouldn't be allowed inside, right?"

Eric shrugged. "Who knows. But I'll help you find her – and we can make her pack up the table as punishment."

Tiffany and Jade both laughed. Sidney didn't have the patience to make pleasantries with them, though. The longer he stood there, the hotter the room felt. His bow tie was strangling him. He needed to get to Rachel as soon as possible, and the more he thought about it, the more overheated he felt.

"It was nice seeing you both, have a good evening."

Eric groaned. "Oh wait – I forgot. I let the valet park me in because I thought we'd be one of the last people to leave."

Sidney realized that he had his fist balled up at his side. He forced himself to release it. His heart was racing – though he realized that the most likely scenario was that Rachel ran off with some friends, she also could've run off with people that she didn't even know. And there was no shortage of people eager to take advantage of a pretty, naive, eighteen year old girl.

An idea flashed through his mind – what if she had been *kidnapped*? It was unlikely, but who knew?

No. That was panic talking. Kidnappers probably wouldn't have taken her somewhere she *wanted* to go, like a nightclub...

"I can give you a ride!" said Jade. "We're on our way out anyway."

Waiting around was killing him. Sidney didn't want to delay another minute if he didn't have to. "I would really appreciate it, if you don't mind."

Jade shook her head. "Not at all."

Eric and Jade continued chatting pleasantly as they walked out to the car. She was parked on the street – quite smart, really. She had no trouble getting out, despite all of the traffic backing up in the garage.

Sidney leaned in from the back seat and gave her directions before settling into his seat next to Tiffany.

"Is Rachel your only sibling?" asked Tiffany.

"No."

After a moment, Tiffany cleared her throat. "I also have a little brother, Connor. And Morgan. She's my half-sister. But luckily, I'm still the oldest."

Sidney glanced at her. It was fine that she was trying to be friendly, but his mind was preoccupied. Rachel wasn't answering his calls and now he was worried she might shut off her phone entirely.

But Tiffany was stuck in the back with him, and he knew that he should at least *try* to be polite since Jade was taking the time to drive them.

"I'm also the eldest. I have a brother, too," he said, not taking his eyes off of his phone. Rachel hadn't moved in a while. That was probably a good thing? "He's two years younger than I am. Rachel is half my age – and she's also my half-sister."

"Wow, that's a big gap – in years, I mean."

He nodded. "It is."

Thankfully Tiffany didn't ask any more questions and there wasn't traffic on the way. They got there quickly and Jade pulled up to the front so Sidney could hop out.

"I'll try to find parking," she said.

"If it takes too long though, we might just be circling the block – so give me a call," said Eric. "I'll hang back."

Sidney nodded and stepped out of the car. He was surprised to see that Tiffany had followed him.

"Oh, you don't have to come with me – I'll just run in and grab her."

Tiffany closed the door to the car and stepped onto the sidewalk. The car behind Jade honked their horn and Jade did a little jump before pulling away.

"No offense, but you might have a hard time walking into this club. Do you see that line?"

Sidney looked up from his phone – he'd been rather focused on making sure that Rachel didn't go anywhere else. There was a line of people that went down the sidewalk and around the corner – as far as the eye could see. Occasionally the door to the club would pop open, the loud music blaring over the voices of the people waiting in line.

"I didn't notice it until now. I don't want to go in though – I just need to check if she's there."

She shrugged. "Suit yourself."

He walked around the line and made his way to the front door where two large bouncers stood, arms crossed.

"Excuse me – I think that – "

"Back of the line buddy."

Sidney sighed. This wasn't really a scene that he was familiar with – he'd never gone clubbing when he was younger. He went once with a friend – no, it was Eric actually. Where was Eric when he needed him?

"I think that my little sister, who was underage, might be inside. I just need to – "

"I'm not going to ask you again. You're way to close, buddy. Step back."

Sidney did as he was told. A few people standing in line jeered at him, yelling "line jumper!"

He turned toward Tiffany; maybe she had some other ideas? He spotted her a few feet away, chatting on her phone.

"Okay – yeah. Tell them I'm here right now. Red dress – yeah."

He took a step closer to her once she put her phone away. "They won't let me in."

"Don't worry. One of my friends from college is a club promoter. I gave her a call – she's going to get me in."

"That's great!"

She crossed her arms. "Unfortunately, I can't bring you with me. But don't worry – I'll find Rachel."

The bouncer who told Sidney to back off was now waving Tiffany over. She turned around and walked toward him, giving him a hug when they met.

Again with the hugging. Was that what he needed to do to get inside? Did he just need to hug the bouncer? Somehow he didn't think that would've worked for him.

He watched as Tiffany disappeared inside.

What if Tiffany couldn't find Rachel? Or what if Rachel really *had* been kidnapped, and this was about to be a scene straight out of an action movie?

He pulled his phone out and saw that Rachel was on the move – seemingly toward him.

He waited by the door, far enough that the bouncers wouldn't yell at him, but close enough that he could see who was coming and going.

Within moments, Tiffany emerged from the club with Rachel at her side.

Relief washed over him like a cool splash of water.

Then came the anger.

"What were you thinking leaving like that?" Sidney said once Rachel was close enough to hear him. "You can't just hop into random people's cars, you could have – "

She crossed her arms. "Yeah, I could've *actually* had fun for once."

"Rachel, this was completely unacceptable, you – "

She huffed and walked past him, standing a few feet away on the sidewalk and texting away furiously.

She was always texting. It drove him insane. Sidney rubbed his forehead and turned to Tiffany. "Thank you for doing that. She's really a handful sometimes. She's not a bad kid but...she needs some direction. How did you find her so fast?"

"Well," Tiffany dropped her voice. "She might've been dancing on top of the bar. So she was easy to spot."

Dancing on the bar? "Great."

"Oh, I see Jade coming around." Tiffany waved and the car slowed down.

"Again – thank you. I really appreciate it."

Tiffany smiled. "And I didn't even need my power suit."

Before he could even open his mouth, Tiffany spun on her heel and walked toward the car.

Sidney felt like he'd walked into a brick wall. Had she heard him make that comment about the power suits? No – she couldn't have. But then...

Tiffany stopped and turned toward Rachel. "Listen Rachel – if you come willingly, I'll give you my number, and when you turn twenty-one, my promoter friend will get you into every club that you could ever dream of."

"Really?" Rachel said, perking up.

"Yeah, I'm a woman of my word."

Amazingly, Rachel turned to follow her and they both got into the car.

Sidney stood on the sidewalk, feeling stunned. His body was finally calming down from the adrenaline, but now he had a new issue to deal with.

Not that it was entirely new – but it was a new realization. Sidney hadn't picked up many habits from his father. He was diligent in avoiding alcohol, and while he lacked the charm that his dad so effortlessly employed, he made up for it with hard work.

Now, however, he realized that he hadn't outrun all of his dad's bad traits – because it was now undeniable that Sidney, too, was terrible with women.

He sighed and walked back to the car.

Chapter 3

The strawberry lemon layer cake turned out *perfect* this year. It was Tiffany's favorite, and Margie only made it for her birthday.

Margie took a step back and admired her work. It was a doozy, standing at over twelve inches tall with alternating layers of vanilla cake, lemon cheesecake, icing, and strawberry jam. She was even able to get fresh strawberries and jam from a farm down the road, and she predicted it'd make all the difference.

This was the first time in a long time that Margie was able to give the cake to Tiffany in person – usually she had to make a tiny version and carefully ship it to Chicago. Tiffany wouldn't take time off of work for something as silly as her own birthday, so Margie found other ways to seize the moment.

But maybe if she made her birthday a positive experience this year, Tiffany wouldn't avoid them so much in the future?

It was worth a shot!

They were expecting a lot of guests for Sunday dinner that day, and Tiffany insisted that her birthday only be a small part of the evening. Margie obliged – begrudgingly. She insisted that Tiffany choose the menu and that they sing at least one round of Happy Birthday.

"I would rather not choose the menu and instead pretend like it was any other day," said Tiffany.

"Nonsense! We have to celebrate you – and celebrate your being here. I promise that I'll keep it low-key."

Tiffany smiled. "All right Mom. It's a deal."

Because of her promise, Margie didn't buy any decorations, noisemakers, or balloons. The most she allowed herself was a beautiful bouquet of flowers that she'd picked up at the farmers market the day prior.

Tiffany gave a few options for dinner, but insisted that she didn't want it to be anything that was difficult to make. Margie didn't mind a challenge, though, and settled on some old favorites: one-pan salmon with roasted asparagus, garlic parmesan fingerling potatoes, and gourmet mushroom risotto.

The risotto was Margie's idea – she knew that Tiffany loved it and it'd been just long enough since she last made it that Margie had forgotten how bothersome it was.

It ended up being a bit tricky, but everything else went smoothly. Hank helped set the table with the new red napkins and placemats that Margie picked up last week.

Red was Tiffany's favorite color, so in lieu of birthday decorations, she could at least personalize the table a tad.

The first guests to arrive were Jade and Matthew. Jade looked nice, as always, and she'd started dressing up a bit more since she'd started dating Matthew. Or was it since Tiffany started living with her?

Margie was unsure – though she did think that Tiffany was playing a hand in at least some of the changes.

"Hi guys! It's good to see you." Margie gave them both a quick kiss on the cheek.

"It's nice to see you too," said Matthew. "And it smells great in here!"

Margie smiled at him. He was always so full of compliments, but not in an insincere way. He was just...sweet. Finally, the type of guy that Jade deserved.

Hank walked in, giving Jade a hug and shaking Matthew's hand. "Just the man I was hoping to see."

Jade raise an eyebrow. "Oh?"

Matthew laughed. "That sounds a little ominous."

"Don't be afraid Matthew," said Hank. "Nothing major. The TV I ordered finally came in and I need a second set of hands to hang it up."

"Oh, that's easy," said Matthew. "No problem."

Hank turned toward Margie. "That is, of course, if we have enough time before dinner, my love?"

Margie waved a hand. "Oh, of course you do. This will be a big help, Matthew, so I don't have to struggle to pick that thing up above my head."

Hank kissed her on the cheek. "I could never let my beautiful bride do that sort of manual labor. This is definitely a job for Matthew."

"Thanks a lot Chief," Matthew said with a laugh.

"I can lend a hand," Jade added.

"That'd be great – you can help guide us."

Margie had just enough time to finish up in the kitchen while they were occupied. It would be nice to get this out of the way – Hank had been talking about this enormous TV for months.

He started with telling her all about the options – the different types of screens, 3D effects, curvature, and the shade (or depth?) of blackness in each pixel. Margie was relieved when he finally ordered something so she wouldn't have to hear about the specifications anymore. And now, if it was hung up, she could sit in front of it and enjoy it like intended.

Hopefully the TV would distract Hank for at least a few weeks before he thought of some other improvement that the house needed.

Margie chuckled to herself – that was unlikely though. The man was full of ideas.

Luke, Morgan, and the birthday girl arrived about twenty minutes later. Margie was just finishing bringing everything out to the table when she heard them come in.

"Hank!" she called out. "Finish hanging up that TV – they're here!"

"Drat," said Luke. "It's too bad that they're all done; I could've helped."

Morgan laughed. "Yeah, I'm sure that you're really torn up about it."

Just then, Hank returned with Matthew and Jade. "Don't worry Luke," he said, slapping him on the shoulder. "We didn't manage to get anything hung up at all. You can help us after dinner."

Morgan burst out laughing and Luke turned toward her, arms crossed. "You could at least pretend not to be so filled with glee that my ploy to get out of helping didn't work."

"Sorry Luke," Tiffany said. "You were a little too obvious with everything. Better luck next time."

Everyone took their seats without too much cajoling; it helped that the food was already on the table. They passed around the plates as everyone except for Tiffany chatted.

Margie frowned. Maybe she didn't like the menu? Or maybe she really *did* want a big birthday party and now felt disappointed?

No – that wasn't like Tiffany. She wasn't someone who struggled with expressing her opinions.

"What's wrong honey? Are you having regrets about the salmon?"

"Oh no!" said Tiffany, straightening in her chair. "Not at all. This is perfect – actually, it's too much, Mom."

"Nonsense! It's not every day that my daughter turns thirty years old!"

She cringed. "Ugh. Don't remind me."

Morgan turned toward her. "Don't tell me that you're going to be one of those women who lies about her age. Is every birthday going to be thirty from now on?"

Tiffany laughed. "No – it's nothing like that."

"I, for one, think it's an achievement," said Luke. "Every year is an achievement. And older women should – "

He stopped talking, likely because of the glare and kick that Morgan launched at him.

It was too late. Tiffany leaned forward, a bemused smile on her face. "Go on Luke. What were you going to say about older women?"

"Not sure what you mean," he said, heaping some potatoes onto his plate. "I would never be foolish enough to utter such a phrase."

Matthew broke into laughter. "Really? Because for a second there it sounded like – "

Hank cut him off. "I think that after dinner, you two fellas need to join me for a serious talk about safety."

"Are you feeling...unsafe Hank?" Tiffany said, sitting back and crossing her arms.

He nodded and took a sip of water. "With these two bozos steering the ship into this conversation? Absolutely."

Everyone laughed. Margie knew that Tiffany wasn't mad – not really. Though she did seem to be going through some sort of quarter life crisis, which was something of a surprise to Margie.

Growing up, Tiffany always seemed to know what she wanted. When she was twelve years old, she started babysitting other kids in the neighborhood – even some who were close to her own age. One of the boys that she babysat was only eighteen months younger than she was! Yet she handled herself so well that no one – neither the parents nor the kids – doubted her.

Her maturity always surpassed her years, and Margie learned early on that the best way to help Tiffany was to offer her advice and then get out of the way. Tiffany was a force on her own, even as a little girl.

She went on to school and excelled in all of her courses. Margie never even had to help her with homework – Tiffany sought out tutors on her own if she felt like she misunderstood information. She landed a competitive internship during college, all without anyone's help, and went on to take a high paying, high stress finance job in Chicago that she seemingly loved.

Tiffany was always strong, and smart, and driven. Now was no different – though it seemed she'd lost her footing a bit.

"I think that's a good idea, Chief," said Morgan. "I know that Luke could use a lot of help."

Luke cleared his throat. "Agreed. All right then, enough about me, does anyone else want to offer their birthday wishes? Morgan?"

"I do," she said, "but before we get into any of the festivities, I have to announce something important."

"What's up?" asked Jade.

"Well I *finally* got word today that my mom's trial is going to start. Jury selection is in a week! On Monday."

"That's wonderful news!" said Margie. "How are you feeling about all of it?"

Morgan sighed. "I don't know. Excited, nervous...angry?"

"I believe that she is feeling all of the feelings," said Luke matter-of-factly. "And I support her fully in these feelings."

Matthew laughed again, shaking his head. But this time he didn't say anything.

"Well, I'll be there every day," said Margie.

"Me too," said Tiffany. "Not that Luke isn't great support but..."

Jade laughed. "He's very good support, but I'll try to see if I can get off of work too."

Morgan shook her head. "No – please don't feel obligated. Though any day you'd like to come to the trial, that'd be nice and I'd be happy to have you. I don't even know if I'm technically allowed to watch the jury selection, but I'm going to be there until they kick me out."

Margie had the urge to get up from the table and hug her, but she didn't want to make Morgan feel uncomfortable. This trial was such a long time coming, and if Andrea found a way of getting away with murder...

It was too horrible to think about. Margie set her fork down. "We'll be there with you, and we'll all be thinking positive thoughts."

Morgan smiled. "Thank you. Anyway – let's get back to Tiffany getting old."

Laughter rippled around the table, even from Tiffany.

"Ha ha. Very funny,." she said.

Margie felt responsible for the birthday teasing and took the opportunity to change the subject. "Girls, I didn't get to hear yet – how were the Milky Way Star Awards?"

"Oh Mom, it was amazing," Jade said, her face lighting up. "I met the director of Great Sand Dunes National Park and rangers from Rocky Mountain and Grand Teton."

"*And* you accepted a huge award," added Tiffany.

Jade smiled. "Yeah. That was another highlight. I hope I can go back every year."

"Well, when you turn Colby's land into a state park, I see no reason why you couldn't attend every year!" said Margie.

Jade nodded, still beaming. "And we saw Eric there, too! I'm really hoping that we get news about the grant funding soon so I can finally tell him that we're going to work with Burke Development to build the park."

"Wait, when did you make that decision?" asked Tiffany.

Jade bit her lip. "Uh...last week, when I met with the committee. We had a vote. And I was hoping that if you talked to him at the awards, you'd be more okay with working with his company."

Tiffany sighed. "Oh come on, I'm not so bad! I'll work with whoever you need me to work with."

"It doesn't seem like you've been Eric's biggest fan," said Morgan.

"I just want what's best for the park." Tiffany shrugged. "And if you think that his company is the best, then we go with them."

Jade smiled. "Do you mean it?"

"Of course."

"So...you wouldn't mind meeting with Sidney to talk about some things?"

Tiffany set her water glass down and stared at Jade for a moment. "I can't believe that you're doing this to me on my birthday."

"I'm sorry! I just – "

Tiffany laughed and put up a hand. "I'm just kidding. Of course. I'd rather work with Eric when possible, though. Sidney is so...arrogant."

"I'm surprised you're willing to work with him at all after what he said about you," said Morgan.

Margie interjected. "What did he say about you?"

Tiffany waved a hand. "Oh you know, just something that showed how afraid he is of a powerful, old woman – as Luke would call me."

Luke cleared his throat and stood up from his seat. "All right then Chief, I believe it's time for us to hang up that television of yours."

Margie laughed and told him to sit back down. "Oh stop it, you. I still have to get the cake! Are you guys ready for some cake?"

There were a few enthusiastic yeses, so as Hank cleared the table, Margie slipped away to pull the cake out of the fridge. She placed a single red candle on top.

It was intentional – she'd only bought one. For Morgan, sure, she would've gone for the comical effect of having thirty candles atop the cake.

But not for Tiffany. One, tall, singular candle was all that she needed. Strong and independent, just like her.

When Margie rounded the corner with the cake in her hands, the group started singing Happy Birthday. Tiffany's jaw dropped when she saw it and sat there, beaming.

Maybe this birthday was a tough one for her, but at least she had all of this love – and teasing – to lighten her load.

Chapter 4

As requested, Tiffany made plans to meet with Sidney on Tuesday. Unfortunately, she couldn't tell him that they'd officially decided on Burke Development yet; they were still waiting on the final letter with the rest of the details about the grant funding. Initially, they were supposed to get the letter before the awards ceremony, but it was delayed for some reason.

Jade didn't want to tell Eric that his company won the bid until the money was in their bank account, but Tiffany thought that they shouldn't wait much longer. Even though Eric was just getting into the park-building business, they didn't want to lose their chance to work with him. Or worse – Tiffany suspected that Eric could change his mind at any moment and move on to something else if they didn't get a contract started.

Sidney suggested that they meet at a coffee shop on San Juan Island. On the one hand, Tiffany didn't want him to make the trip *just* to meet with her. But on the other hand, her savings were quickly dwindling, and she didn't need to spend money traveling to Seattle if he would come to her.

As she got dressed, she made sure to wear an outfit that would be less intimidating to Sidney; instead of a "power suit," she wore a simple, professional black dress and two inch heels.

It was one of the tips she'd learned from Vera, an older colleague at her previous job. Vera was nearly thirty years her senior and at the beginning of her career, she was often the only woman on any team she worked on. She was sharp and tough, yet always kind.

Tiffany loved working with her – she was super cool and didn't take crap from anyone. And she offered advice in much more straightforward ways than others ever did.

"Tiffany," she once said, "you're a good looking woman."

She remembered laughing at this and replying, "If you're trying to flatter me, Vera, it's working."

Vera kept on talking. "It's not a good thing; in fact, it'll often hurt you. Some people think beautiful women are stupid. They'll talk down to you and not listen to your opinions. Others might think you've only gotten where you are based on looks. Some men will only give you the time of day if they think that you're interested in them, and this will lead to women getting jealous."

"Whoa, I'm not *that* good looking," Tiffany said.

"It doesn't matter. You can't let any of it get you down. But you also can't ignore it. You have to be twice as good to prove these people wrong and walk with your head held high. Got it?"

Tiffany let out a sigh. Vera's advice served her well for many years, and this meeting with Sidney was no different. Sidney was by no means a flirt, but he clearly had a low opinion of her. Maybe it wasn't because of her looks – though he did mention her clothing.

It didn't matter what his problem was. She'd put on her best professional face and kill him with kindness – and skill.

She took a look at herself in the mirror and realized that she was missing something – her birthday necklace from Morgan. She grabbed it from her dresser and put it on. The chain was the perfect length, long enough to hide under her dress if she wanted. But she liked showing it off – the charm was a beautiful, intricate compass. Morgan wrote in the birthday card that she knew Tiffany would find her way, but a little help now and then never hurt.

Tiffany had almost choked up when she'd read it. Her thirtieth birthday was much more emotional than she'd expected it to be, but her mom was right – being with family made it much more bearable. Enjoyable, even.

They were supposed to meet at the coffee shop at noon, but Tiffany decided to get there ten minutes early so that she could get a good table.

To her surprise, Sidney was already there when she arrived. He'd set up in the back with a large laptop in front of him and papers scattered around the table. It looked like he'd been there for hours.

It was her own mistake; she wouldn't let him pull one over on her again. Next time, she'd be an hour early.

He stood up when he saw her approaching. "Hey Tiffany, it's good to see you again."

She shook his hand. "You too."

"Please, have a seat," he said. "I'll see if I can get the barista over here – I apologize, I didn't know what to order for you."

"That's all right." She watched as he struggled to get the attention of Sam, the college student who'd taken Luke's position.

After a moment, Sam waved at her and called out from across the coffee shop. "The usual Tiffany?"

"Please!"

She took a seat.

Sidney cleared his throat and tidied up some of the papers around him. "Thanks again for meeting with me today."

"Thank *you* for coming out here. I do appreciate it."

"Of course."

She set her purse on the seat next to her. She had her laptop in there, but she didn't think it was time to bust it out yet. "How's Rachel doing?"

"Quite well, and thank you again for your help."

She smiled. "Anytime."

"I haven't had much of an active role in her upbringing, until recently," he said. "My stepmother – her mother – filed for divorce from my father. And she reached out to me to help with some things."

This sounded like some interesting family drama. "Just as Rachel became a handful?"

He turned back to his computer, a small smile appearing on his face for the briefest moment. "I suspect she's been a handful for some time, but yes."

He handed her a folder, and she opened it and removed the thick packet inside. "It's nice of you to take her under your wing."

He nodded, but was clearly ready to move on from this conversation.

"Here are some of the updated figures that Eric mentioned last week."

Tiffany started leafing through the packet, but her mind wandered. She didn't remember hearing much about Sidney's father – only Eric's father.

Eric's dad, Dan Burke, started Burke Industries; but they'd never heard so much as a peep from him about the Colby project. It seemed that the new branch of the company, Burke Development, was under Eric's control – for the most part. Sidney was always hovering around, his disapproving face ever present in the background.

"Hang on a second," she said. "What does this say here?"

Sidney leaned across the table. "I think that's from the environmental impact report?"

"Right, but it says that there's no expected cumulative impact on any sensitive species at the development site."

"I'd have to check the report, but..."

Tiffany nodded. "Yeah, double check that. Because I'm pretty sure that's not right. Yeah – actually I'm sure. There's a list of six trees that we were encouraged to plant and preserve."

Sidney clicked around on his computer and after a moment said, "Oh, I have it right here. You're right."

Tiffany suppressed a smile. She'd read that report multiple times – she could probably recite it if she needed to. She loved stuff like that – she loved the details and the parts that other people skipped over.

"Is there anything else that looks out of place?"

"Not yet," she said as she continued to read the packet.

"Let me give you my card so if you find any more issues you can email me directly," he said, reaching into his pocket. "Eric put together some parts of this document and...I'll be going over them again."

Tiffany slipped his card into her purse. "Sounds good."

"I'm assuming you haven't heard anything about the grant?"

She shook her head. "Unfortunately, no. But we're expecting to hear from them any day now."

He nodded but said nothing.

Tiffany let out a sigh and set the packet down. "We don't have the money yet, so I really shouldn't be telling you this, but Eric basically won the bid. Jade loves his plans – she loves the cabins, the recreation center, the camping area and that indoor pool that he engineered."

"That was actually my idea," he said.

"Oh. Well – it was a good one. And his designs with the staggered buildings and floor-to-ceiling windows for ocean views – it's all really incredible."

Sidney smiled. "Eric does have great ideas. And a wonderful design team, of course."

"Of course." She was about to pick up the packet when she paused again. "So, Jade is sold. And I agree that Eric has exciting plans – but I want to hear from *you* why you think we should go with Burke Development."

Sidney sat back and looked at her for a moment before responding. "Let's be honest – you and I both know that there haven't been any other legitimate development proposals for this park. So really, we're not your *best* option – we're your *only* option."

Tiffany tried to force herself not to smile. He was *alive*! Now she was intrigued...

Chapter 5

"Is that right?" Tiffany said, completely unmoved. She had the tiniest bemused smile on her face – not gloating, but playful.

Sidney smiled. "I'm sorry, but it is."

Tiffany sat back and crossed her arms. "You must've done some extensive research into the subject."

"My research is always extensive," he said with a shrug.

She nodded slowly, taking a sip of the coffee that the barista had just dropped off. "Then you also know that there are *seven* other major, well known outdoor developers in the Northwest, and each company has no less than six years experience – with three of those companies having done work on Washington State Parks in the last year."

Sidney kept his expression neutral. He knew that – sort of. Well, he'd only known about five of the other companies.

And he hadn't checked who had been working in parks recently. His comment was meant to be a playful jab – though he knew that there was at least some truth to it.

Apparently, Tiffany took playful to a new level.

"Therefore," she continued, "whether or not you're right about being our best option, it doesn't mean that we couldn't have more options, if we so choose. So again, Mr. Burke, I ask why you think that your company would be the best choice for our project."

He couldn't help it – he chuckled. "Fair point, Miss Clifton."

He reached into his bag and pulled out another packet – one that he initially didn't think he'd have to talk much about. But it seemed that he'd underestimated Tiffany. He had no idea what her background was, though; he made a mental note to look her up online later that day.

"I thought that you might say something like that," he said. "I prepared a statement detailing our team, our financials, and our goals. And I'm happy to go over all of that with you."

She nodded, eyes darting over the first page.

"Let me summarize," he said. "I understand that this project is very important to your sister. Well – and I will go over all of the details here and answer any questions you have – but my main point is that this project is extremely important to my cousin as well. His father, my Uncle Dan, is allowing Eric to take charge of his own branch of Burke Industries. And while I'm helping him with this – "

"Lucky you," Tiffany said, smiling broadly.

Sidney studied her for just a moment; she was also far more intuitive than he initially gave her credit.

He continued. "Eric is in love with this project. And we need it to work, probably even more than you and Jade need it to work, so that we can launch his business properly."

Her eyes met his and he paused to give her a moment to speak, but she said nothing.

"So yes, while I'm aware of our competitors and the fact that they have vastly more experience in this type of development, I don't believe any other company has as much passion, nor as much at stake as we do."

Tiffany set the papers down. "Well then. I think we can work with that."

The meeting didn't last much longer; they only had about forty minutes before Sidney had to leave. He now regretted that he scheduled a meeting with their plumbing team so early in the day.

He would have preferred to spend more time talking to Tiffany and getting to know her motives. Was it possible that she knew about these other companies because she was pursuing them too? Maybe she was just using Burke Development for ideas...

It was impossible to tell. She was stunningly well-versed on not just the environmental impact report, but also a slew of regulations and permit issues that were anticipated for the build.

They'd had the sort of conversation that Sidney could only *dream about* having with Eric; the best he could do was hold Eric's attention in twenty to thirty minute blocks. He had to simplify all of the information and sometimes even make checklists to make sure that Eric understood what he was talking about and that they were in agreement.

But with Tiffany it was like...talking to an expert. Sure, there were some things that she didn't know, things that she couldn't possibly have known, unless she had been working in development for years. But her attention to detail, and her knowledge of the reports and plans was unbelievable.

Sidney even considered postponing his next meeting so that they could keep talking, but he knew that the group would be busy in Oregon for the rest of the week, and he didn't want to make the flight out there. Instead, he promised to email her later that evening with some specific numbers that she'd had questions about.

As he sat in the plane back to Seattle, his head was spinning. Where on *earth* had Tiffany come from? If he didn't know any better, he would've thought that Tiffany was some sort of attorney or developer hired to represent San Juan County.

He pulled out his phone and searched her name online. Her photo popped up right away. No, she wasn't an expert or plant from the county – she definitely shared a last name with Jade. She was family. They looked like sisters, too.

Sidney navigated to Tiffany's LinkedIn page and looked over her extensive resume. He paused when he saw the employment section – could that be right? It looked like Tiffany had been unemployed for a few months.

Interesting.

Was she fired? Had she quit? Did she take leave so that she could help Jade with this park?

Now *that* was family devotion. If Tiffany thought that he was doing a lot for Eric, it was nothing compared to her quitting her career to help her sister.

He let out a sigh. If anyone understood family devotion, it was him.

He wasn't sure exactly how he ended up as Eric's right hand man, but he was happy to help. Eric *needed* his help, and it was natural for Sidney to step into that position. He'd spent years working under Uncle Dan on a variety of unglamorous projects: apartment buildings, business complexes, parking garages.

Not the stuff of glossy magazines, but they were important things. Complicated builds with permits and zoning and schedules.

And now Uncle Dan, despite having a soft spot for his only kid, was starting to lose his patience. He made it clear that even a hint of failure would cause him to cut off all funding to Burke Development. And when they were alone, Dan told Sidney that this was on his head, too.

There were days that Sidney wished he could send Eric away on a vacation or something, just so that he could have more control of the project. Eric was putting all of his eggs in one basket, convinced that they *had to* do this park. He said it would put their name on the map.

"C'mon Sid! To *be* big, you have to *think* big!" he'd say.

Sidney understood that it was exciting and new. But was it necessarily the smartest job, or the best one to start with?

He wasn't sure about that, but he was willing to support his cousin. Was it possible that the combination of Eric's exuberance and his own experience would be a perfect match?

Maybe.

Besides all of that, Burke Development was important to Eric, and by helping him, Sidney had a chance to repay his uncle for everything he'd done throughout the years.

It wasn't just that Uncle Dan taught him all about the business; he was also a refuge and never-ending source of kindness while Sidney grew up – particularly when, as a moody teenager, Sidney struggled through the chaos of his dad's alcoholism.

Uncle Dan never lost his patience with either of them, even though Sidney's dad was forever having ups and downs. His dad was a good guy – really and truly – but he had a demon that he just couldn't shake. The highs and lows were tough for everyone, but particularly Sidney's mom, who left when he was young.

For years, his dad managed to keep jobs here and there, usually by the grace of Uncle Dan. But now it seemed like the alcoholism was swallowing him whole, and even Dan couldn't tolerate his unstable behavior.

The last straw was when Sidney's dad crashed his car into the downtown Burke Industries office building. Dan was forced to acknowledge that it was unsafe having him around and told him he had to leave – for good.

His dad didn't take the news well and said he'd never forgive his brother's "betrayal." By that point, Sidney had seen so many of these tantrums that he was unfazed.

Yet it did seem to be a breaking point – his dad hadn't had a good day since his final dismissal from Burke Industries. He stopped making house and car payments. He stopped taking care of himself. And that was when Rachel's mom filed for divorce.

It all barreled downhill, and he disappeared. Sidney hadn't talked to his dad in over a year.

He let out a sigh. He couldn't dwell on it; he had a lot of people still counting on him. Uncle Dan, Eric – even Rachel, though she'd hate to admit it.

He suspected that Tiffany was not *so* different than he was. He finished up the rest of his day as quickly as possible, feeling excited to get home and send the documents to her. Just as he was sitting down to his computer, though, his phone rang.

Eric!

"Hey buddy, how's it going?"

"Not good man," Eric said.

"What's up? If you're worried about my meeting with Tiffany, don't be. I think it went really well and we're going to be a good team."

"I don't doubt it," said Eric. "But Jade just called me – in tears. She said – this is unbelievable – that the Washington State Parks Department just announced that they're bankrupt."

Sidney felt his mind freeze. "What?"

"Yeah. Which means they don't have the money to fund the grant."

Sidney closed his eyes. "Right."

"What're we going to do? I can't believe this! I thought that..."

"Don't panic," said Sidney. "We'll figure something out, okay?"

"Don't tell my dad. Please. Not yet."

"Yeah, I know. I won't. We need to come up with a plan. Let me think."

"All right. Thanks Sidney."

He set his phone down and looked at the email he'd started to write to Tiffany. If there was anyone who might have a contingency plan, it was her.

He changed the subject line to, "Bad news" and wrote out a message.

Chapter 6

The initial news that the grant wouldn't be funded sent Jade into shock. Then she quickly went through all of the stages of grief – denial, anger, and bargaining.

By Saturday, though, she was firmly in the depression stage. She'd investigated a dozen other possible grants and revenue streams for the park, but nothing was going to work. Either they had already missed the deadlines, their park was too small to qualify, the requirements were too strict for their current plans, or they had to go through an extensive process that would take a year or longer.

Basically, they needed to start from zero. Again.

Matthew had to work, but he stopped over before his shift and brought her a bouquet of flowers. She tried to invite him in for a cup of coffee, but he'd unfortunately already gotten a call that he needed to respond to.

"But tomorrow I *insist* that I'm taking you out to dinner and getting your mind off of this," he said.

Jade sighed. "You don't have to do that. Just spending time with you is enough."

He looked up for a moment as though he were contemplating it. "Nah. We're going. Somewhere nice, too. You always deserve special treatment, but especially now. Think about where you want to go, okay?"

"Okay," she said with a smile before closing the door after him.

The flowers were beautiful – his mom had taught him well. Stuck to the bouquet was a card that read, "My love – these flowers are only a glimpse of the beauty that you will put into that park. I believe in you. Forever yours, Matthew."

Jade reread the card three times before tucking it into her pocket. She'd started scrapbooking and saving all of these little things from their relationship: cards, ticket stubs, pictures.

She was sentimental that way, and she thought that maybe one day, she might even have someone to share all of these pretty scrapbooks with. Maybe...their kids?

The first time that Matthew brought up kids, Jade was surprised. It was casual, like it just popped out of his mind.

He'd said, "I like where I'm living now, but I'm hoping to save up and buy a house in a year or two. You'll have to approve of it, of course. And it'll need to have a much bigger yard for kids."

He could have just said that he needed a yard for his dog Toast to run around in, or for barbecues or something. But no – he said that she'd have to like it *and* it had to be good for kids.

Her heart sang in these moments, but she didn't always know how to react. Matthew made no secret of his feelings, but sometimes it took Jade a bit longer to put her thoughts into words. Luckily, Matthew didn't mind – if she was smiling, he'd just wrap his arms around her and give her a hug.

She put the flowers in a vase in the kitchen and tucked the card into her most recent scrapbook.

"Oh la la! Are those from Matthew?" asked Tiffany.

Jade nodded. "Yeah. He feels bad about the grant stuff."

Tiffany sighed. "Don't we all. I'm guessing he didn't have any ideas?"

"No, unfortunately not."

Jade's phone buzzed in her pocket and she pulled it out to see who was calling.

Shoot! It was Dad.

She bit her lip – normally, she'd answer, but she didn't want to do that in front of Tiffany. But if she didn't answer, then he might just keep calling and...

She stood there, frozen.

"Well, are you going to pick that up or what?" asked Tiffany.

She had to stop acting suspiciously. Jade pulled the phone out of her pocket and answered the call as she stepped into her bedroom.

"Hello?"

"Hey Jade! It's me."

"Hey Dad, how are you?"

"I'm good, I'm good. I just had Tiffany's birthday present returned to me in the mail though – do you know if she changed her address?"

"Oh...I didn't realize that you didn't know but...she's living here now."

There was silence for a moment before he responded with, "Oh. Right."

"Yeah, I'm sorry, I just thought that..."

"No, I knew. I just forgot. And she hasn't been answering my calls."

Jade took a seat on her bed. If Tiffany knew that Jade still spoke to their dad...well, she wouldn't be very happy about it. "Yeah."

He let out a sigh. "Listen, I know I've made a lot of mistakes. But she won't even give me a chance to explain myself."

"Well to be fair, Dad, you've never really *tried* to explain yourself before," Jade said, as gently as she could.

"I know but...things are different now. *I'm* different now. Let me prove it – I think I can help you guys."

"That's really okay, I think that – "

"No, really. There's something not right about this bankruptcy declaration. Something weird is going on at the Washington State Park department."

Now he had her interest. "What do you mean?"

"I've been an accountant all of my life, and something's just off. And I can help you. Please – if you let me."

"I'll think about it," she said. "I'm sorry – I have to go."

"All right, but let me know. And I'll send Tiffany's present to your address."

"Okay."

She ended the call and opened the door to her bedroom to find Tiffany standing there, arms crossed.

"Were you talking to Dad?"

Busted. "Yeah, he asked me about your address because the birthday present he sent you was returned."

Tiffany laughed. "Oh yeah. Well – news flash. I've blown up my life."

"He said that you're not taking his calls, so I thought – "

"Of course I'm not taking his calls! I can't believe that you *are*. Well actually – I can believe that you are. You think everyone can be saved, don't you Jade?"

Jade shrugged. "It's not like that. But I feel like if he's making an effort, I'm not going to push him away. He said things have changed and he wants to explain – "

Tiffany put up a hand. "I'm good, thanks. And what if Morgan found out you were talking to him? Wouldn't she be heartbroken, after how he treated her? And her mom?"

Truth be told, Jade worried about that a lot. "I don't know. Possibly."

"I mean, do what you want to do. But I'm not going to talk to the man."

Jade nodded. Tiffany discovering that she was still talking to their dad actually went better than she'd expected. Maybe Tiffany would be interested if she heard that he wanted to help? "I told him about the grant losing funding. He thinks there's something fishy with the bankruptcy."

She rolled her eyes. "Yeah, and if anyone would know about fishy financials, it would be Dad."

"I think his business has been bad recently," said Jade. "Like – *really* bad."

"Yet he wants to give us advice?"

Jade shook her head. "No – he just wanted to help us look into it. But I'm getting the feeling that you're not interested in his help."

Tiffany laughed. "I'm sorry, I'm not." She paused for a second. "But...I hadn't even thought of it from that angle before. I've just been looking for alternatives, but what if something fishy *is* going on? It takes a crook to know a crook."

Jade frowned. "I don't think Dad's a crook."

Tiffany shot her a look. "Let's just say that his 'business' was always in the gray area between legal and illegal. And actually..."

"What?"

"Remember that threatening letter that we got? That said that we needed to be careful?"

"Yeah." Jade frowned. "It said 'it doesn't end with Jared,' or something. But how could Jared have his claws in the parks department?"

"I'm not sure...yet." Tiffany shrugged. "But Sidney sent me an email – he seemed like he didn't want to give up. Maybe I'll see if he has some time to talk?"

Jade clasped her hands together. "Oh, would you? But wait – actually, if he's mean to you, I don't want you working with him."

Tiffany shook her head. "Oh, don't worry about that. He's not mean to me. And I'm not afraid of him. In fact, I like the challenge."

Jade smiled. Tiffany had come back from that meeting extremely energized. Perhaps Sidney was a good match for her...intensity? "Okay then. I'm excited to see what you can do!"

Chapter 7

Since it was Saturday, Tiffany wasn't sure that Sidney would even respond to her email. But it was worth a shot. She decided against mentioning her dad's theory, and offered to meet over a video or phone call so that he wouldn't have to travel again.

She got her answer within twenty minutes. He wrote that he was happy to swing by Friday Harbor again.

Impressive!

Or was he a workaholic? Answering an email in twenty minutes on a Saturday seemed like something Tiffany would have done at her old job.

No matter. Tiffany wanted whoever worked on Jade's park to be serious. He alluded that he needed to come to San Juan that Sunday anyway. Still, he was being nice.

Or...did he just not trust her to handle anything on her own? That might be the case.

To be fair, she'd never worked outside of finance. It was all new to her, and if he thought she was incompetent...oh well! All she could do was keep trying her best. She hadn't done *too* badly so far, and no matter what, it was none of her business what he thought of her.

Though it still annoyed her that he'd insulted her. She paused. Had she fallen into her old patterns? Did she secretly want to prove him wrong?

Yeah, of course! Okay, so maybe it wasn't *so* secret. Maybe it pushed her to work twice as hard so he couldn't catch her on anything. Tiffany had always taken strength from situations like this – she enjoyed the challenge.

What she needed to focus on, though, was that this project was really important to Jade. No matter how Tiffany felt about it, or what people thought of her, Jade deserved her full attention. Plus, it was literally the only thing that Tiffany had going on at the moment. She had no excuse for doing a bad job.

At work, she used to juggle multiple projects and clients all the time. What was *one* little park project? Even though this was an entirely new type of "job," Tiffany didn't feel out of place. And she wouldn't let Sidney get in her head.

The next day, Tiffany didn't make the same mistake with getting to the coffee shop. She got there an hour early this time and was very pleased to see that Sidney hadn't yet arrived. She ordered herself a drink and set up her laptop so that she could continue researching the parks department budget.

Surprisingly, Sidney did not arrive extra early.

Five minutes before he was supposed to get there, Tiffany took a chance and ordered a black coffee so that it could be waiting for him when he arrived. It was something she learned over the years in working with clients. She tried to remember everything – their coffee order, the names of their kids, where they like to vacation.

She truly enjoyed getting to know people, and remembering details was important. She didn't know anything about Sidney, though. Not really. All she knew was that it seemed like he liked drinking black coffee and scowling at everyone.

He arrived promptly at two o'clock.

"I'm so sorry I'm late," he said as he took a seat.

"You're actually right on time."

"Well, I tend to think that fifteen minutes early is on time. But being *actually* on time..."

"Ah, of course. You do seem like the type to be extremely hard on yourself."

He paused. "Do I?"

"Don't read too much into that." She said with a smile. "It takes one to know one. I ordered you a coffee – just black. I hope that's all right?"

He looked down, a flash of surprise registering on his face. "Oh yes, that's perfect. Thank you."

Good, not only had she beat him to the coffee shop, she even got his order right. This was all going to help her convince him of her theory about the parks department. It would be no easy task, especially because she didn't have any real evidence of her suspicions.

"So have you found any alternative funding?" he asked, taking a sip of coffee.

"Unfortunately I have not. Neither has Jade, or anyone else on the committee. It's been a glum week on San Juan."

He frowned. "I'm sorry to hear that. We haven't been able to find anything either."

"I started thinking..." She pushed a pile of papers toward him. "Where did this bankruptcy situation even come from?"

He picked up the first page as she pointed out some of the highlighted items.

"Here are some of the meeting minutes from the last year. And on page eighteen, you'll see a news story from six months ago where a millionaire died and left half of his fortune to the Washington State Parks department."

"And how much was that?"

"Two hundred *million* dollars," said Tiffany.

Sidney raised an eyebrow. "That's quite a sum."

"Yeah, I thought so. Especially because that covers the park budget for an entire year, not even counting the thirty or so million they get as taxpayer support. So, they got a bunch of money that they weren't expecting, and somehow they already spent it all? How does that work?"

Sidney kept flipping the pages. "Yeah – and it looks like last year, they earned one hundred and twenty million dollars in revenue."

"Exactly! Are we supposed to believe that they just *forgot* to collect campground fees and parking passes for the entirety of last year? Or that they had some huge hole in the budget – something that's never really mentioned in any of the meeting minutes?"

"I'm assuming you read all of them."

She nodded. "Yes. And sure, there are different proposals here and there, but nothing that would drain all of that money! It's just very...weird."

Sidney was now flipping through the pages much more quickly. "This is brilliant – it really is. I don't know what we can do with it yet, but you're right. Something is off."

Tiffany had to force herself not to beam at him like an eager schoolgirl. Not only was he on board with her thinking, but he was even enthusiastic! It seemed like no small victory to have Sidney Burke in such ardent agreement.

"What are you thinking – as far as next steps?" he asked.

Tiffany sighed. "I'm not sure. This week is going to be really busy for me."

He set the papers down and sat back in his chair. "Oh? Interviewing other companies for the build?"

She laughed. "No, but if I told you what I was doing, you wouldn't believe me."

"Try me."

Did he really need to know? But then again, she didn't want him to think she was untrustworthy if she wouldn't tell him. She cleared her throat. "I'm attending a murder trial."

He didn't flinch before saying, "Oh. Who did you kill?"

Now she couldn't help it – she burst out laughing.

Darn it. She thought that she'd be able to keep an upper hand in this meeting. But oddly, she got the feeling that Sidney wasn't easily bested.

Chapter 8

Oh good. She liked that one.

He never knew how people would take his humor – sometimes, they couldn't tell that he was kidding and they thought that he was just making fun of them. That was always awkward.

Sidney got his sense of humor from his mom. She was always so funny, and she could deliver anything with a straight face. It was that sense of humor that got her through many difficult years with his dad.

"Very funny," Tiffany said. "But no, it's...I mean honestly, you're not going to believe me."

"I might."

After a moment, she said, "A woman is on trial for a hit-and-run murder of my half-sister Morgan's mother."

He put up a finger. "Hang on – let me follow that. Your half-sister's mother?"

Tiffany nodded. "Yeah, we share a dad. And not a good one."

Sidney considered saying something about his own dad – but what was there to say? He couldn't put his thoughts together quickly enough. "I'm sorry to hear that."

"It's fine. Actually – this is so dumb," she laughed. "Oh, what the heck. He's the one who brought up the idea that there might be something wrong in the parks department budget. I feel like I should tell you this as a disclosure or something."

He set his coffee down. "What do you mean, a disclosure?"

She sighed. "He's just – he's had this accounting firm for most of his adult life, and apparently it's failing now. I don't know the details – I don't want to know. I've already spent a lot of years in therapy talking about him."

Sidney froze – he didn't know how to respond. Now would be the perfect time to mention his own dad – but he didn't know how.

"I'm sorry, I don't mean to bring this all up," she said quickly.

"No, it's not that. I can imagine that..." He paused. "Well, honestly, it's hard to imagine that he's worse than my own dad. So please, go on."

She smiled and thankfully continued talking. "I don't know the details, but he called me for my birthday and was going on about something not being right – actually, he called my sister."

"Your half-sister?"

She shook her head. "No, sorry. He called Jade. We only met Morgan a few years ago – we didn't know that he'd had an affair when we were all little."

Sidney nodded. "Ah, I see what you mean about the therapy."

"Yeah. And anyway, you could probably read all about this in the news, but Morgan's mom was killed by – excuse me, *allegedly* killed by – this oil baron's daughter, Andrea Collins."

Her face twisted when she said the name.

Sidney mirrored her look of disgust before adding, "Ew, Andrea."

She paused. "Oh shoot – I'm sorry, do you know her?"

"No, I don't think so. And if I did know a murderess, I'd hope that we wouldn't be friends."

"I hope so too, Sidney." She crossed her arms. "Would you say that you're a good judge of character?"

"Yes," he said before realizing that she was likely referring to the comment she'd overheard at the Milky Way Awards. He tried to add, "I mean – "

She waved a hand. "Well anyway, I don't know why she's a crappy person, but she is. Maybe it was growing up rich, or beautiful, or being called princess one too many times by her father."

"Your dad never called you princess?" he asked, trying not to smile.

"Do I *look* like a woman whose father called her princess?"

He laughed and shook his head. "I don't know, I'm afraid to answer now."

"You can't be afraid of me Sidney, we're a team! But long story short, basically, I'm going to be a bad member of our team this week. I think I'll be spending a lot of time in the courtroom, supporting Morgan."

"I'm happy to pick up the slack. I have a friend who's a forensic accountant, actually."

"Really?" She leaned forward. "That sounds pretty interesting."

"It seems to be, yes. I can ask her to look into some of this for us – to see what she can find."

"That would be really helpful, thank you Sidney."

"Of course."

Sidney had to meet with someone from the zoning board. He was sad to cut their meeting short – though he didn't know how many meetings he would need before he could talk as frankly about his own father as Tiffany did about hers.

Actually, no. It was too soon in their business relationship for him to talk about his dad. Or would it ever even be appropriate? He couldn't talk to her about his family's problems; it just seemed wrong.

It was so uncomfortable, and once that information was out there, he couldn't take it back. What if someone then used that information against him? As open as Tiffany seemed to be, it could all just be a persona built from years of experience in business.

Perhaps it was all part of her plan to keep him around. Sidney felt a bit iffy about going to this meeting with the zoning board. There was now absolutely no guarantee that the project could even go forward; why was he still putting time, money and effort into it?

He knew that realistically, he should be pursuing other options as aggressively as possible. Except that wasn't what Eric wanted to do...and now it wasn't what he wanted to do, either. He believed in Jade – that was for certain. And now he was even starting to believe in Tiffany.

Was it worth the risk?

He had no idea. He didn't have much experience with risk; that was more Eric's department. Sidney didn't really have the luxury of taking risks, because he never had a wealthy family to fall back on. Sidney never had money of his own – well, not until recently when he started becoming successful in Burke Industries.

For years, Sidney was just barely scraping by. He saved carefully and was frugal in every way. His car was twelve years old! He did most of the work on it himself. Uncle Dan was always embarrassed when he tried to take that car to meetings and insisted that he take the company car instead.

But Sidney wasn't embarrassed; he was proud of how far he'd come in the world. He wanted to instill some of that pride into Rachel, but it seemed like everything he did fell on deaf ears. He had no idea how to catch her interest, though he'd be happy if he could even figure out how to avoid her disdain.

Anyway, things were a little more secure for him now. It wouldn't ruin him even if Burke Development had to pull out of this project in a few weeks. He'd convince Eric to move on, somehow. And they could build somewhere else.

Truth be told, Tiffany was keeping him guessing. She so casually mentioned that murder trial, as if it were the most normal thing in the world. Maybe all that therapy helped her in being so candid?

Sidney had no idea where to even start the story of his own family drama. Tiffany would be horrified if she knew the truth. While her father might be a cheat, his father was...something else. Sidney's relationship with his dad, and the man himself, was far more complicated than a simple chat over coffee could summarize.

He'd come a long way since being under his father's thumb, though. Sidney could afford to take a risk on Jade and her inscrutable sister, at least for a little while. And maybe clever Tiffany was worth it?

Chapter 9

The first day of the trial was on Monday, and though Morgan tried to prevent scheduling any work stuff for the week, there were still a few things that needed to be taken care of. Luckily, Luke was happy to take care of them for her.

Initially, he wanted to cancel everything so that he could go with her. But the first day or two of the trial was just going to be jury selection. How come they never showed that part on TV?

It didn't matter, it was all working out fine. Her dad wouldn't be in until Tuesday, and Margie would keep him busy – probably by overfeeding him. She'd insisted, of course, that he stay at her house. He tried to resist, but Margie threatened to call and cancel any reservation he made elsewhere. Morgan told him there was no use in refusing her forceful hospitality, and he finally gave in.

Hopefully they'd get to hang out after the trial. For now, it was perfect that Tiffany was able to tag along for jury selection. Morgan wasn't sure what to expect, and Tiffany always looked like she belonged, no matter where she was. She was a great partner.

Jury selection started early, and Morgan was ready to go by seven. It was a bit overkill to get up so early, but she couldn't sleep. All night, she woke up because of nightmares and fears that she'd oversleep her alarm.

She spent her spare time in the kitchen waiting for Tiffany, who *finally* emerged from the bathroom at 7:28.

"Okay Tiffany! Let's get going."

"Sorry, I thought you said we were leaving at eight?"

"No, jury selection *starts* at eight. And we need to get there early enough that we can get a seat in the back so that we don't attract any attention."

Tiffany looked her up and down. "Is that why you're wearing a baseball hat and sunglasses? Or are we going to rob a gas station on the way there?"

"No, I got gas yesterday so that I'd be ready," said Morgan.

Tiffany cracked a smile. "I didn't mean – "

"Oh – stop! I don't want them to see me! What if they kick me out?"

"Don't worry," Tiffany said, putting her hands on Morgan's shoulders. "I asked my lawyer friend – he said it's kind of weird but technically you're allowed to be there. Okay?"

Morgan took a deep breath. "Okay. Are you ready?"

"Of course! Let's go."

They drove to the courthouse and had no problem finding parking. Morgan kept her hat and sunglasses on until they were safely in their seats; once inside, Tiffany convinced her it was more suspicious to keep them on.

There were a lot of people in the room, but before long, Morgan realized that most of the people were possible jurors – not spectators like she was.

She leaned over and whispered to Tiffany, "Okay, who do you like for the jury? That lady over there has a nice face."

Tiffany squinted. "The younger one or the older one?"

"The older one." Morgan paused. The younger one didn't look nice at all – she had her arms crossed and her lips were pursed like she was sucking on a sour candy.

"I can see that." Tiffany nodded. "The older lady looks like a grandma who knits things and bakes a lot of cookies."

Morgan nodded. "Yeah! That's *exactly* the kind of juror that we need."

"At first, I thought you meant that other girl – the one with the stink face."

Morgan smiled – Tiffany had noticed too. "No. She could still be nice, I guess. Maybe her face is just like that."

"Very possible." Tiffany lowered her voice. "Someone once told me that *I* have a stink face."

"You do not have a stink face."

"It's okay, I know I do," Tiffany said quietly. "It's really at its worst when I'm thinking about something."

"Then stop thinking so much. Problem solved."

Tiffany smiled. "And stop being scary?"

Morgan nodded. "Definitely. I mean, you're the scariest one in the family."

Tiffany turned to her, eyes wide. "No! Scarier than Chief Hank?"

"Oh, big time! Honestly I was more intimidated by you than I ever was by him."

"Are you serious?"

"Shh!" Morgan shot her a look. "Keep your voice down, scary! We're going to get in trouble."

Tiffany shrank down. "Sorry!"

"But yeah, you have that effect on people."

Tiffany crossed her arms and sat back. "Darn it. I have so much to work on."

"Why would you want to change that? Isn't that sort of a cool skill, to be intimidating?"

"No!" Tiffany whispered. "I don't want to be the scary one! I want to be the…"

"Go on."

She bit her lip. "I was going to say nice one, but that's Jade. I don't know what I want to be, but not scary."

"You'll figure it out."

More people started to fill into the room and Morgan felt uncomfortable taking up a seat – she told Tiffany that they should probably get up and stand in the back. She didn't want to be confused as a potential juror.

Tiffany volunteered to get coffee for them both and Morgan stayed behind to watch everyone. There was still nothing going on and people were starting to chat. There was one guy who was loudly bragging that he was going to say whatever he needed to say to get out of having to serve jury duty.

Morgan had a hard time not saying something to him, like, "Sorry that my mom's murder is such an inconvenience to you." But she knew that would immediately start a loud fight and get her kicked out of the room, so she kept her mouth shut.

Luckily, Tiffany came back soon after, and Morgan got to quietly vent all of her frustrations to her. Tiffany offered to go over and tell the guy he was free to go.

"That way, he'll be out of our hair, and he'll also get in trouble for not showing up."

The idea made Morgan laugh, but her temper had calmed down. "Nah. It's fine. He doesn't know this is my mom's case, it's not personal."

"Right. He's probably a butt head all day, every day."

Morgan smiled. "Exactly."

After nearly two hours, things finally started moving. The group was asked a few questions and they had to answer by raising their hands. Morgan watched carefully as the first possible juror stood and was taken off to the side.

He was a man in his late forties who looked less bored than some of the other people. And less annoyed. Was that a good thing? Morgan wasn't sure.

She strained to listen to the kinds of questions they were asking him. Things like, "Do you or anyone you know work in law enforcement?" and, "Have you ever been the victim of a crime?" and, "Is there any reason why you couldn't be fair and impartial if you are selected for this case?"

He answered no to all of the questions, and apparently he was deemed acceptable.

Morgan turned to Tiffany. "Well, that was easy. One down and fourteen to go."

"I thought there were only twelve jurors?"

"There are. But they have two alternates."

"Look at you, little trial pro."

Morgan smiled but said nothing. She felt so powerless; all she could do was learn about the trial process and hold on for the ride.

The next person called up was a woman who looked about Margie's age. She seemed much less cooperative than the first guy, and she answered "yes" to one of the questions.

She was deemed *not* acceptable, but was sent back to sit down and wait with the rest of the jurors.

"Nice try lady," said Tiffany. "She probably thought she'd get to go home early if she was difficult."

Morgan sighed. "I guess so. But we also don't want anyone on the jury who doesn't want to be there. They need to listen to all of the evidence and make an informed decision."

Tiffany reached out and patted Morgan on the knee. "Don't worry, I'm sure they're pretty good at picking people."

"Yeah." Morgan knew they must be – but then why did she feel so sick?

The entire process was taking much longer than Morgan anticipated. When she heard the questions a couple of times, she felt like she knew them by heart. She kept watching all of the potential jurors carefully, but now she found it a bit easier to keep up a conversation with Tiffany.

"So how's your new job hunt going?"

Tiffany rubbed her face with her hand. "Oh. You know, not well. Because it's not going at all."

"How come?"

"Because...I don't know what to do with myself. And I feel like I don't even know what I want anymore."

"I know you're in a tough place. But I really admire you."

"Really?" Tiffany narrowed her eyes. "Are you messing with me?"

Morgan shook her head. "No, not at all. You realized that your life wasn't heading in the direction that you wanted, and you actually did something about it. A lot of people just give up. Half the battle in getting where you want in life is being able to admit to yourself when you're going the wrong way."

Tiffany leaned back against the wall. "Hm. That's really nice of you to say."

Morgan watched as Tiffany pulled a necklace out from under her shirt.

"Is that why you got me this compass necklace?"

Morgan smiled. "Yes! It's a token for your future."

Tiffany squeezed her hand. "I love it. Thank you."

"Aw, really? I'm glad you do. I know that you usually like fancier stuff, but – "

Tiffany cut her off. "Fancier stuff! That's not true. I'm just...really bad with money. I spend it all."

They both laughed.

Tiffany continued. "I really love it. And I hope you're right and I figure out where I'm going."

"You will. I believe in you." She paused for a moment, listening to the questions being asked of another potential juror. This guy was giving all "No's," he seemed like he might get a pass. She cleared her throat. "I think you have to focus in on what your values are."

Tiffany frowned. "I'm not even sure I know what you mean."

"Oh come on, of course you do."

She sat for a moment before responding. "Nope. No idea."

"Well, what's most important to you, and how does that guide your life?"

"Morgan," Tiffany said with a groan. "First the compass, now these questions about values? When did you decide to be the deep sister?"

Morgan laughed. "I'm not trying to be deep. It's just when my mom died, I had a lot of regrets and time to think and..."

"I'm sorry," Tiffany said after Morgan trailed off. "I didn't mean to make you talk about this."

Morgan shook her head. "No, it's okay. I miss my mom like crazy – like every day. And I know it's cheesy, but life is so short. We can be snapped away at any moment, and we don't have the luxury to live in violation of our values."

"Wow. When you put it that way..."

"Just think about it. Like, some of my biggest values are creativity, bravery, family, and...hope."

"Those are really good ones. Can I just use those?"

"Sure, but I bet that you have some other ones too. There are huge lists that you can look at, and you can go and rank your top ten or whatever."

Tiffany pulled out her phone and searched "life values." After a moment of scrolling, she asked, "What do you think Jade's values are?"

Morgan crossed her arms. "Good question. I'm sure family is one for her. And I bet she has a bunch that I don't have – like empathy. And gratitude."

"So you're saying that you *don't* care about empathy and gratitude?"

"Yes, that's exactly what I'm saying." Morgan laughed. "Kidding. It's just that...yeah, I think those things are important, but I don't make life decisions based around them, you know?"

Tiffany shook her head. "I feel like I'm going to end up with a list of fifty things and feel really inadequate if I can't do them all."

"I bet that one of your values is ambition."

"Yeah, that sounds right. Isn't that one of yours?"

Morgan shook her head. "Not really. I think I value creativity more than ambition."

Tiffany frowned. "I can say for certain that I don't really care about that one – creativity."

"See! Just go home and think about it. It'll be really interesting."

It was time to break for lunch and everyone started to leave the room; they stood waiting as everyone passed. Morgan watched Tiffany, who was quietly scrolling through the list of values on her phone.

Morgan could see that Tiffany was struggling, but she had full faith in her. It was all a new experience for her; she was not someone used to failure. Not even in the slightest task.

How funny was it that Tiffany didn't realize how ambitious she was? And how obvious it was to others.

Morgan was often guilty of not seeing herself the way other people saw her, but Tiffany *really* didn't realize how she came across. To the outside world, Tiffany was put together, sharp and professional.

How was it that she didn't see that in herself? It almost seemed like Tiffany had a poor understanding of herself because she didn't spend much time thinking about others.

Not in a selfish way or anything. It was odd – Tiffany didn't give much attention to what other people were doing. She was simply disinterested and instead she was always focused on her own goals and ideas.

In some ways it was good; Tiffany was is no way a gossip or nosy. It was like she had better things to do – until now. All of a sudden, she was slowing down and starting to look around. And she was completely surprised by everything that she saw.

It was funny to Morgan, and she enjoyed being there for Tiffany's revelations.

Most of all, she was thankful that Tiffany was there with her. As they walked out to lunch together, Morgan knew that she had a true ally. No matter how this trial went, she knew that in the end, she wouldn't be alone.

And maybe if they were lucky...Andrea would be found guilty and justice would be served.

She decided to savor that hope and focus on the present moment. Tiffany accepted her offer to buy lunch, and off they went, arm in arm.

Chapter 10

The jury selection dragged on into Tuesday. Tiffany went along with Morgan again, bright and early, so that they didn't miss anything. It was fortunate that the last juror was selected before lunch; Tiffany could see the cracks starting to form in Morgan.

She'd hardly slept the past two nights and had started keeping detailed notes on all of the jurors. When they got home for lunch, Tiffany gently tried to take the notes away from her, but Morgan snapped them back and clutched them to her chest.

"These are important!" she protested, eyes wide and wild. "We need to keep a running log of what each juror is thinking."

"Morgan," Tiffany said gently, reaching for the papers again, "even if you know what they're thinking, how is that going to help? You can't talk to the jury. You know that, right? You can't show up at their homes or start emailing their family members."

Her grip remained firm. "I know. I don't want to intimidate the jury, I just..."

Tiffany raised an eyebrow. "You just what? Want to look like a mad woman with a stack of weird, hand written notes about a bunch of strangers?"

She frowned. "That's a very ungenerous view of what I'm doing."

Tiffany stood, arms crossed and saying nothing.

"I just..." Morgan shifted her weight, but didn't loosen her grip at all. "I want to feel like I have a little bit of control."

"And I get that, but just promise me one thing?"

"What?"

"That you won't spend the entire evening scribbling on these papers! Can I take you out, can we do something? I'll do anything you want, I'll even go for a bike ride."

Morgan laughed. "Wow, you must be *really* desperate to get me away from this insanity if you're willing to exercise."

"I never said I would be happy about it," Tiffany replied.

"I really appreciate it, but Luke is already a step ahead of you." Morgan paused. "He's taking me to a pottery class and then to dinner."

"Oh, that's good. It'll keep your hands busy, at least."

"Yeah. And I hope you're not mad, but he bought tickets for Jade and Matthew too."

Tiffany thought for a moment before responding. "Why would I be mad?"

She sighed. "Because he's a doofus and didn't get one for you, too. But I'm sure I can talk them into letting you – "

Tiffany put up a hand. "Please, don't worry about it. I'm not mad at all. I don't really like...activities like that. Messy, artsy things."

Morgan laughed. "Okay, but will you join us for dinner after?"

"Sure, that sounds fun."

"Okay great. And actually, I only have about an hour before I have to leave for the class. So if you don't mind, I think I'll excuse myself to be alone with my crazy thoughts."

Tiffany stepped aside. "Be my guest!"

Tiffany went into her bedroom, shut the door, and laid flat on the bed. She closed her eyes for a moment; it would be nice to take a nap, but that felt irresponsible somehow. She'd never been a person who took naps before, but then again, she never had so much free time on her hands, either.

She pulled her laptop over and opened it. There was still a window open with a list of over two hundred life values.

She'd scrolled through them last night after talking to Morgan, but felt oddly overwhelmed by the idea of picking out a list to define her life. Instead, she left the tab open on her computer (and phone) and looked at it every time she was going to do something else.

It was time to stop avoiding it. She pulled out a sheet of paper and spent half an hour creating a list of twenty-five values that she thought were most important.

How was she supposed to pare them down further, though? Wasn't that the idea, to have a top three or something?

Or was it more like she kept them in the back of her mind, and when she was making a decision, she had to run through her values and made sure that it made sense? Even for that, twenty-five seemed like too many. How could she be sure that a decision to accept a job, date someone or move somewhere satisfied all of those values?

It seemed like Morgan had a much easier time narrowing down her list. Tiffany laughed to herself thinking of Morgan dismissing empathy as a value. It wasn't that Morgan wasn't an empathetic person, though – so obviously there had to be some cuts.

Tiffany had never thought about these sorts of things before. How had she gotten to thirty without thinking about this stuff? She was so frustrated with herself. Supposedly, she was a smart person – yet somehow she allowed this to happen.

Maybe Morgan was right and half of the battle was realizing and admitting to herself that she wasn't going in the direction that she wanted. She'd spent so much of her life motivated by nothing but...anger. She wanted to show people who doubted her that she would succeed. She needed to show her dad that she didn't need him.

That anger only got her so far.

And now what? All she could do was put her energy and copious free time into what was happening around her. For once she wasn't thinking of what she wanted; she was thinking of what was important to the ones she loved: Jade's park project, and Morgan's trial.

Actually, she hadn't had much time to think about the park project while they were in court, so maybe now she could do some investigating.

It made her angry to think that there was even a chance that some sort of budget shenanigans could cost Jade her park. Tiffany would do whatever it took to get to the bottom of it.

She was reading through more department meeting minutes when an email popped up from Sidney.

Perfect timing!

The subject was, "Good news?"

She smiled. His emails were always like that – a hint in the subject, as though he felt like he needed to entice her to actually open the email. Of course she was going to open it – who else was as convinced as she was that there was some sort of fraud going on within the parks department?

She quickly read through it. He had some information that he wanted to share with her, and he wanted to know if she was free that evening? He said that he could pick her up in Friday Harbor if she'd like to go for "a little boat ride."

My my, it wasn't just Eric who liked the theater of a surprise.

Tiffany started writing her response immediately – she was interested in hearing his news. But the boat thing...what was she going to say about that?

Was he trying to show off, or something? Maybe not – he might do this with all of his clients.

Or maybe he wasn't trying to impress her at all and he was going to show up in some small, rinky-dink boat. But that didn't seem like Sidney's style.

She decided to agree to the boat ride, but made a point not to ask any questions about it. For her to make assumptions about his intentions was...wrong.

It was something that the old Tiffany would have done. By trying to figure out his motives, she was reacting in the way that she always used to – arising from a feeling that Sidney thought poorly of her, and trying to prove him wrong.

Perhaps it wasn't personal at all. Perhaps the man just liked boats.

She didn't want to be the old Tiffany. After Malcolm's death, she wanted nothing to do with that Tiffany or that way of living. After he passed, she felt so hollow, and like the earth had been pulled from beneath her feet.

Nothing made sense to her for a while; but now she was trying to piece it all back together. Life was a beautiful and deli-cate thing, and even the people who seemed like they had it all together weren't portraying the full picture. If scowling Sidney wanted to chat on a boat, who was she to judge?

Tiffany let Morgan know that she'd be missing dinner "for important parks business," and that evening, at six o'clock, she waited at the edge of the Friday Harbor Marina.

There wasn't much activity at this time of day; the most excitement was a whale watching tour that unloaded about twenty bright-faced sailors onto the docks. Apparently they must've seen something good, because their laughter and loud voices filled the air as they filed past her and back into town.

The water looked positively dreamy at this time of day. A few clouds floated by, in seemingly no hurry, matched by the slow movement of the boats in the distance. She closed her eyes for a moment and enjoyed the warmth of the sun on her face.

Tiffany looked at her watch – Sidney was ten minutes late. If his intention was to impress her, he was *not* succeeding.

"Oh hey – I didn't see you there!" said a voice behind her.

Tiffany spun around to see Sidney standing there, a coffee in each hand. He was dressed much more casually than she'd seen before – she'd never seen him in anything but a well-fitted suit.

Now, though, he had on dark pants, boat shoes, and a white button-down shirt. The wind had tousled his hair a bit and he looked very...cute.

Tiffany was startled to see him, but perhaps even more startled by his just-walked-out-of-a-sailing-magazine look.

"Oh – I'm sorry, I don't know how I missed you," she said. "I've been here for like ten minutes."

"I'm sorry – that's my fault. I got here a bit early and thought I would grab us both something to drink."

"Thank you." She accepted the cup from him. Had taking that suit off knocked something loose? He seemed more relaxed; he was even smiling!

She took a sip of the coffee. "Hang on – how did you know to get a vanilla latte?"

He smiled. "It was easy – I just asked for your regular."

"Ah, very clever Mr. Burke."

"Are you still interested in a voyage this evening?"

"Yes, of course."

He smiled and turned toward the dock. "Then follow me."

They walked past all of the large boats, bobbing in the water, until they arrived at a small, rubber raft-looking type thing.

"After you," he said, offering a hand to help her down.

"Thanks," she said. Well – she was wrong about him trying to show off. This certainly was not a boat used to impress anyone.

Though Tiffany *would* be impressed if she didn't fall over the side and drown; she carefully navigated into the boat and tried to sit down as gracefully as possible. No need for this new, rugged sea-faring Sidney to think she was a klutz.

He hopped in after her, untied the boat, and started the engine. She didn't know how they were going to have a conversation; the engine was so loud. Maybe once they got out further they could turn it off and be able to hear each other?

Or maybe that was the entire point of this boat! Maybe what they were talking about was *so* confidential and dangerous that they had to make sure they weren't being listened to...

No. That didn't seem right. She'd listened to too many true crime documentaries.

"Where are we going?" she asked.

He pointed over her shoulder. She turned around to see that they were headed for an enormous, stately yacht. Tiffany had never been on such a huge boat before – it must've been fifty feet long!

"Oh!" She exclaimed. "That was not what I expected."

"Did you think that I made it all the way from Seattle in this little dinghy?"

Tiffany laughed. "I guess not? I'm not well-versed in ships."

"This raft is so small that I don't think you can even call it a ship," he said. He approached the yacht and parked the dinghy perfectly before again offering his hand to help Tiffany onto the larger ship.

She was happy to accept his help, because she foolishly chose to wear heels. They weren't terribly tall, but they still made her more unstable than she liked. The skin on his hand was rougher than she'd expected – and his grip was strong and reassuring. She made the transition with ease, and Sidney carefully passed off her drink.

"Well," she said. "It'll be much easier to drink my coffee without spilling it on *this* ship."

He shook his head. "I can't believe that you thought I was going to drive you around in that little raft. How low is your opinion of me?"

She shrugged. "It's not really my opinion of you, but my knowledge of sailing."

"Fair enough," he said with a nod.

"Is Eric a sailor too?"

Sidney finished securing the dinghy and stood up. "Not exactly. He likes riding around on boats, though."

"Interesting."

Sidney crossed his arms. "Why is that interesting?"

"I just assumed that sailing was something you were taught in boarding school, or whatever."

A smile spread across Sidney's face. "You think that I went to boarding school?"

She studied him for a moment. "You didn't?"

"No. Public, all through high school, then the University of Washington for college."

"Oh." Well, that was awkward. How was she supposed to know that the Burke cousins had such different upbringings? Although it did make sense, if she thought about Sidney and Eric...

He led her onto the deck. "It all makes sense...if you think that I'm a spoiled rich kid."

Tiffany set her coffee down and took a seat. "Well, you did just pick me up in a fifty foot yacht."

He laughed. "True, but it's not mine. It's my uncle's. My father wasn't as successful as Uncle Dan. My father struggled – well, he *still* struggles – with alcohol. Really, most of what we had growing up was because of my Uncle Dan."

Tiffany's eyes locked onto his. He was still smiling, but it was a sort of melancholy smile. It suddenly hit her that he had a good reason for his ever present scowl. "Oh wow, I'm sorry, I didn't mean to make assumptions about – "

He put up a hand. "It's all right. It's not a big deal, but it's important to me that you know where I came from."

Tiffany stared at him for a moment. What did he mean by that? Why was it...important to him?

After a beat, he added, "If we're to do business together, I mean."

Oh. For a moment there, she could've sworn that he was...being vulnerable, or something.

She was reading too much into things. Maybe she'd allowed her idea that Sidney might not despise her to go to her head. He wasn't interested in her in *that* way – he didn't like her *or* her power suits!

He was just a great businessman, trained by his uncle, apparently. And he happened to look really good whether he was in a suit or a simple white button down shirt...

But that was neither here nor there.

She cleared her throat. "You've just never said much, so I made some assumptions. And now I feel pretty silly, so I'm sorry about that."

He smiled and she felt a flutter in her chest.

Oh dear. This was *not* how she was supposed to feel toward her new business partner.

Chapter 11

"We all make assumptions in business," said Sidney, taking a seat across from Tiffany. "You have to. At least the first time that you're working with someone – every collaboration, to some extent, is a leap of faith."

Tiffany nodded. "Yes, that's true."

That was a good save on his part. She seemed to buy it – the business aspect of their relationship.

In truth, he had never spent this much time with a client. Maybe Uncle Dan was more open like this?

No, not like this. He was much more of a schmoozer than Sidney could ever dream to be, but he wouldn't tell a beautiful client his life story.

Sidney's reasoning, though, was that he'd initially made a very poor impression on Tiffany – especially with his loud blunder, where he was overheard making a rude comment about her. Now he wanted to work with her and get to know her and...well, it was just important that she knew some things about him.

"My father, Ryan Burke, is three years younger than Dan. Dan was always protective of him – he still is, really. But it was Dan who was the driven one, and the one who started a very successful company in Seattle."

"Burke Industries, right?"

Sidney nodded. "Right. My dad was never driven like that. While Uncle Dan was building this empire from the ground up, my dad went to college – for a bit. But he dropped out. He learned a bit about art and history, and even more about tequila and vodka. In a lot of ways, my dad is a beautiful soul. But the alcohol has always been his dark side."

Tiffany shifted in her seat. "You said that he's still around?"

"He is. Why?"

"I just wasn't sure why you have so much...responsibility for Rachel."

"Ah. Well, it's a long story. My dad met my mom in college. She was also a free spirit – they were both kind of hippies in their time. They got married, had me and my brother, and tried to make it work. But it never did work – not for long, at least. When I was ten, my mom left."

Tiffany set her coffee down. "Oh my gosh, I'm so sorry."

"It's all right. At the time I didn't understand, and I directed all of my anger at her. But it was complicated, as it always is. Once I was older, we reconnected and I found out that she tried to get custody of us, but it was impossible. My dad had expensive lawyers and she had nothing – she didn't have a stable job, and she hadn't been able to finish her education."

"Are you closer now?"

Sidney cleared his throat. "We reconciled, yes. But she passed away a few years ago, from a heart attack."

"Oh," Tiffany said softly.

He continued. "After she'd left us as kids, I began to get the full brunt of my dad's blackouts. He could go a week or a month like that – where he turned into a completely different person. And then, all of a sudden, something would change. He'd wake up one morning and be himself again."

"Wow. And you were *ten*?"

Sidney nodded. "I tried to protect my little brother as much as I could. And Uncle Dan – he did what he could, too.

When my dad was sober, he'd give him work. He thought that if he could help him succeed that it would help him turn his life around."

Tiffany frowned. "But that didn't work."

"No. He married my stepmother when I was eighteen, and Rachel was born. By that point, I was focused on making sure that my little brother got into school and was able to move on with his life. I lived at home for the first two years of college and commuted so that I could keep an eye on things. But as soon as I could, I got an apartment for me and my brother and left it all behind."

"Well. And here I thought you were sailing at boarding school."

He laughed. "You're not entirely wrong. Eric did have the sort of upbringing that I think you're imagining – boarding school, an Ivy League education. And...I love my cousin. He's a great guy, and there are benefits to that sort of an education."

Without missing a beat, Tiffany said, "But there are also benefits from the sort of education you received."

Sidney paused for a moment. Most of the people that he worked with had no idea about his background – they assumed that he was Ivy League bred like his cousin.

In those instances, it was better not to correct them; if they knew about his humble beginnings, he would lose some credibility. He would be viewed as an outsider in a world of elites.

But not with Tiffany – she was different than the people he'd grown accustomed to working with. And he'd unfairly turned his cynicism onto her before he even got to know her.

Sidney smiled. The least he could do was try to make up for it now by telling her about his past. "You're right. After I left, I cut contact with my dad for a few years. Apparently, it was a sort of wake-up call for him. The next decade was perhaps the best of his life – he hardly drank at all and had very few binges. He got more involved with Burke Industries and started making money. A lot of money."

"Uh oh."

"Yeah. We made up, to an extent. When my stepmother asked for a divorce, it was the beginning of a new spiral."

"I see. And what's he doing now?"

Sidney shrugged. "I'm not entirely sure. I talk to him once in a while, but it's scattered. His mind isn't all there; I think the years of drinking has taken its toll. I want to help him, but he's never wanted help. He gets angry. It's...a difficult relationship. But, he did ask me to help take care of Rachel."

"So she has become your half-sister, and your ward."

"Yes." He laughed. He'd never thought of her as a ward before. "Which she *fully* resents. But with the way that my stepmother spent Rachel's inheritance, she has no option but to listen to me. Occasionally."

Tiffany laughed. "Nothing like the venomous sharp tongue of an eighteen-year-old girl to keep you on your toes."

"Exactly. If you have any advice, I'm happy to take it."

"I'm sorry, I can't say that I have much advice. Though I suppose, if this is a period of full disclosure, I should tell you what I was like when I was eighteen. Though I didn't have the tumultuous sort of upbringing that you had."

"That's quite all right," he said. "It's not a competition."

"As you know, my father is a crook and he was not around much when I was growing up. I spent many years in therapy getting over this and putting together the woman you see in front of you here today."

Sidney smiled. He knew she was making a joke, but she looked *quite* good to him.

She continued. "My mother is a wonderful, loving, saint. I have my sister Jade and my little brother Connor. And of course, my newly discovered half-sister Morgan, who my father abandoned before she was even born."

"Top-notch dad behavior," said Sidney.

"Yes. I had a full ride to college, where I studied finance, because I foolishly believed that it was a path for go-getters, which I was convinced that I was. I worked at several firms in New York City before taking a position in Chicago, where I devoted many eighty hour weeks to making other people very, very rich."

Sidney raised his eyebrows. He had to pretend that he hadn't looked up her entire employment history online. "Oh."

"I nearly had my MBA finished when my friend and coworker Malcolm was diagnosed with terminal cancer. The company to which he devoted his life responded to his darkest hour by firing him and forgetting that he ever existed."

The word cancer knocked the wind out of Sidney's lungs. "That's awful."

"It was." She nodded and her expression softened. "And a few weeks after he died, they promoted me. And then...I handed in my resignation."

Sidney sat back in his seat. "Wow. And that's what brings you here today?"

"Yes. I am a thirty-year-old career woman with no career, unless you count making up conspiracy theories about the Washington State Parks Department."

Sidney laughed, heartily. Her honesty was a bit off-putting to him initially; it seemed too cutting at first to be genuine. But he was more and more convinced that it was real. "Well, I guess you had to put all of that go-getter energy somewhere, eh?"

"Indeed." She looked around, seemingly admiring the ship. "So you said that this *isn't* your yacht?"

He nodded. "Yes. It's my uncle's. He never got a license for boating, or learned how to drive, so I did. That way I could tag along to important client meetings and observe how he worked."

"Very impressive Mr. Burke," Tiffany said, standing up. "Now what was it that you wanted to show me?"

"Oh – follow me. I have some papers in the cabin."

"Your uncle has great taste," Tiffany said as she followed him. "But I can't even dream how much the ship cost him."

"Neither can I," Sidney replied. "But I'm guessing it will rival the bill for Rachel's college tuition."

Tiffany laughed. "It's too bad that that's probably true."

She took a seat in the cabin and Sidney handed her a folder containing a stack of papers. He felt like he was always handing her stacks of papers, which oddly, she was always excited to receive.

"Excuse the thrown-together appearance – I was trying to make all of this while working with my accountant friend. Basically, she found some suspicious activity. But unfortunately, nothing that we can connect yet."

Tiffany looked up from the papers. "Yet?"

"Let me show you." He leaned in closer so they could look at the page together. Her perfume smelled so lovely. Was there a chance that she'd put that on because she was meeting him? Or did she wear it every day... "Do you see this timeline up here? This is the day that that millionaire announced he was donating all of that money to the parks department. The *very* next day, a super PAC was formed, called 'Washington Beauty Keepers.'"

"Wait, like a political funding group?"

"Yeah."

Tiffany frowned. "Why does that sound so gross?"

He laughed. "Well, because the group so far has funded candidates who want to do the *opposite* of keeping beauty in Washington. They've given money to politicians – from both sides, mind you – who are interested in cutting back on regulations, like logging in Washington State Forests or selling off plots of state parks."

"So their purpose is the opposite of the name of the group."

"Right. And you'll never guess how much money they've given out."

"Um...is it two hundred million? That was donated to the parks department?"

"Well – almost. One hundred and twenty million, so far. All in the past few months."

"Wow. And it was started the day after the parks department donation announcement? By who? And who's donating to it?"

He flipped to another page. "That's the problem. All of the contributors so far are from these weird organizations that don't exist – they're offshore shell companies that aren't linked to any actual people."

"That is all super weird," said Tiffany.

"I know. I mean, this group has donated more than almost all of the other groups combined. That's all my friend found so far, so it's not much to go off of. It doesn't prove anything but it's just...weird."

"Yeah, exactly." Tiffany flipped back and forth, looking through some of the information about the candidates who were supported by the super PAC. "Yet if you look, every one of these people does *not* want to keep Washington state beautiful. This guy wants to change the law so that the killer whales around San Juan Island could be captured and sold to aquariums!"

Sidney nodded. "Yeah. The only thing these people want to keep beautiful are their pockets, lined with money."

"What can we do next?" asked Tiffany. "After this trial is over, I can really dive into all of this. It's just this week that's bad for me."

"I understand. I'm going to keep looking, and my friend will too. I'll let you know if I find anything."

Tiffany was still furiously flipping pages. "This is really great. There's definitely something here. I can feel it."

Tiffany continued to be completely enthralled by the papers in front of her, and it gave Sidney a chance to study her for a moment.

It wasn't his intention to get her history by sharing his own, though he did appreciate her opening up. Everything that she'd told him seemed very straightforward and honest; he was now regretting that he ever doubted her, or suspected that she was playing the field with other contractors.

He just wasn't used to people saying what they meant like that. Just as Tiffany wasn't used to wealthy developers not having come from money.

He certainly didn't hold it against her, because his first assessment of her wasn't too kind either. At least now she knew the truth about him, and perhaps would see him in a better light.

"We can talk out some ideas tonight. I've mapped out a trip around the islands, too – depending on how much free time you have this evening. Sunset isn't until nine o'clock, so we still have some daylight if you'd like to sail around a bit."

Tiffany set the papers down and smiled. "That sounds really nice."

"I've got some food upstairs as well. We can make this a real...working-sailing dinner?"

Tiffany tucked the folder into her large purse. "Sure. That sounds perfect."

Sidney had to force himself not to smile so much. If only all of his work dinners were this charming.

Chapter 12

"Honey, I don't think we're allowed to eat anything in the courtroom."

Margie frowned. "What's the chance that anyone will even see? Besides, what if they're hungry? I'm just going to bring a few snacks in my purse."

Hank laughed. "If you say so. Is it a giant purse day?"

"Oh, you *bet* it is!" Margie pulled her bag from the floor and set it on the table. It already held five bottles of water, a box of granola bars, and several Ziploc bags of cookies that she'd baked that morning.

Hank took a peek inside. "Actually not as bad as I expected. May I carry that for you, my dear?"

"I didn't know you were such a fan of the big purse," said Margie with a smile.

He leaned down and kissed her. "I'm a fan of you not throwing your back out and having to sit in an uncomfortable courtroom chair all day."

"Well, if you insist." She handed it to him and planted a kiss on his cheek.

Margie appreciated that he didn't make any more comments about her purse. She had a lot of nervous energy and she didn't know how else to deal with it.

Firstly, she was worried about Morgan and her dad Ronny having to face Andrea in court for the first time. Margie was also worried about Jade, who had been so busy with work and also so sad about losing her grant funding that she'd hardly said much the past week. Margie was also worried about Tiffany, who seemed to be dragging through a quarter life crisis that she didn't want to discuss.

All of these issues felt more pressing now that the trial was upon them; it was like Margie had hit her limit for stress and it was pushing her to a breaking point.

She let out a sigh.

Deep breaths.

For now, she needed to focus her attention on the trial. And if that meant sneaking several unnecessary pounds of food into the courtroom, so be it.

The plan was for everyone to meet at the courthouse, and once Margie was satisfied by the breakfast sandwiches she'd prepared, she went and gently knocked on the door to the guest room where Morgan's dad Ronny was staying.

The door popped open right away. "Good morning Margie."

"Good morning Ronny!" She was happy to see that he was ready to go. He probably couldn't sleep either. "I made some breakfast sandwiches – they're in the kitchen, and whenever you're ready, we can get going."

"Oh, thanks Margie. I'm not really a breakfast kind of guy – I'm sorry. Maybe I'll pack one up for later?"

She nodded. "That's a really good idea. I'll pack them all up!"

After wrapping the sandwiches in foil and adding them to her giant purse, they all piled into Hank's truck and headed to the courthouse. When they arrived, the crew was already waiting – Jade, Morgan, Tiffany, Luke, and Matthew.

Margie felt herself starting to get emotional at this scene, especially when Morgan gave her dad a long hug. She didn't want to cry, so instead she reached into her purse and started passing out breakfast sandwiches.

"They're still warm!" she said. "Eat!"

"Mom," Tiffany groaned. "We can't just stand outside eating like a pack of wild animals!"

"Speak for yourself," said Luke, his mouth full. "If I'm going to testify today, I need all the strength I can get."

Everyone laughed. Normally, Morgan would make some sort of comment teasing him, but today she was quiet.

Food couldn't solve every problem, but Margie thought it was at least worth a shot. She reached into her purse and handed Morgan a bag of cookies. "Here sweetie – you hang onto these. They're your favorite."

Morgan smiled and accepted the cookies. "Thanks Margie. And thank you all for coming. I think I'm going to go inside."

They all watched as Morgan and Ronny went into the courthouse.

Margie turned to Jade. "How's she doing?"

"Okay, I think?" said Jade. "As good as could be expected, I guess."

Luke finished his sandwich and threw the foil into a nearby trashcan. "I better go in, too. Thanks Margie."

"We'll all go – finish up everyone!" Margie said, hand extended to collect the leftover foil.

They took their seats and continued chatting. The courtroom was filled with people, many of whom Margie had never seen before; nothing this dramatic had ever happened on San Juan Island. At least not since she'd lived there.

Margie watched as the prosecuting attorney, Leo, took a seat at the front table. When the defense attorney came in with Andrea, a hush lulled over the courtroom.

Andrea walked in, head held high, and took her seat at the front. There actually seemed to be a team of attorneys surrounding her, but the oldest and seemingly nastiest one was Rudy, a smug-faced man who was smiling and laughing as though he'd just walked into brunch.

Margie felt a bump and looked to her left.

"Try not to glare so *openly*," Hank said.

She laughed. "I'm sorry. I'm just so...*ugh!*"

"I know honey," he said putting one arm around her shoulders. "I know."

When the judge entered the courtroom, they were all instructed to rise. Margie couldn't believe it was all really happening!

Judge Gore spoke after being introduced. "Court is now in session. We call case number 803, the state of Washington against Andrea Collins. Is the prosecution ready?"

"Yes your Honor."

"Is the defense ready?"

"Yes your Honor."

"We will now hear opening statements from the prosecution."

"Thank you." He stood from his chair, moving to face the jury. "Your Honor, and ladies and gentlemen of the jury, my name is Leo Metz and I represent the state of Washington today."

Margie was impressed already. She didn't know much about Leo, though Hank told her that he was a good sort of guy. He could have moved on and up in his career, but he preferred to stay in San Juan County. Hank at least seemed to believe that he knew what he was doing. She hoped that he was right.

"Over the course of this trial, we will present to you the evidence that Andrea Collins is guilty of vehicular homicide. We will show that Andrea, after a night of drinking and fighting with her boyfriend Brock, took off in Brock's 1963 Corvette Stingray. We will show you the video surveillance of Andrea driving to Friday Harbor on the night of the homicide, as well as the bumper that she left behind at the scene of the crime, after she brutally ran over Kelly Allen and left her to die."

He paused for a moment and Margie realized that it was so quiet, she could've heard a pin drop.

"You will get to hear the testimony from the responding officer and how he discovered Kelly that night, a beloved mother and wife, discarded as an inconvenience. You'll get to hear from the man that Andrea confessed her crime to, before trying to flee the island to escape justice. With all of this, we will prove that Andrea is guilty of the murder of Kelly Allen. Thank you."

He took a seat and Margie reminded herself to take a breath.

"Thank you counsel," said the judge. "Would the defense like to give their opening statement now, or would they like to defer until the prosecution rested their case?"

Rudy stood from his chair. "We would like to give our opening statement now, your Honor."

"You may."

Rudy buttoned his jacket and smiled warmly, turning to the jury. "Your honor, and ladies and gentlemen of the jury, I'm

Rudy Vale and I represent the defense of Andrea Collins in this case."

He clasped his hands together and paused to look at Andrea. "My client is being accused of a crime that she did not commit. Yes, a horrible accident occurred on the night that Kelly Allen perished. And yes, someone did leave her, hurt and defenseless that night. But that person was not Andrea Collins.

"My client is only guilty of being at the wrong place at the wrong time. The prosecution will try to show you that by even being associated with a car, she is guilty of murder. They will try to argue that this accomplished, talented young woman was somehow responsible for a horrible tragedy. But we will aim to show you the truth, and ask for a verdict of not guilty. Thank you."

Margie was stunned by the arrogance of Andrea's attorney; how could he argue that Andrea was an accomplished, talented woman? And anyway, what did that matter? She was also a murderer!

He took a seat and the judge spoke again. "Thank you counsel. Will the prosecution please call their first witness?"

Leo first called on the officer who responded to the 911 call. He was sworn in and took his seat.

"Officer Iams, can you tell me what happened on the night of Kelly Allen's death?"

He nodded. "I was on patrol that evening and got a call about an injured person found down on the road."

"What time did you receive that call?"

"I believe it was just before 8 PM."

"When you arrived at the scene, what did you find?"

"I found the victim, Kelly Allen, unconscious and bleeding in the road. I searched the area for evidence as the paramedics tended to her, and I located a detached bumper."

A picture flashed up on the screens in the courtroom. "Is this that bumper?"

He nodded. "It is."

"And was there anyone at the scene? Anyone who admitted to causing the accident, to hurting Kelly?"

He shook his head. "No, there was not."

"So whoever caused her injuries had left the scene."

"Correct."

"Thank you Officer Iams."

Judge Gore motioned toward Rudy. "Would the defense like to cross-examine?"

"No, Your Honor."

Officer Iams was dismissed and Leo called his next witness, the coroner.

Hank had warned Margie that this would be a difficult part of the proceedings; pictures of Kelly would be shown for the courtroom and the jury, and he suggested that they not look at these pictures.

Margie followed his advice and kept her eyes downcast for the entirety of the coroner's testimony, only stealing a few glances at him as he spoke. Once the pictures were up and he described Kelly's injuries, the prosecution began to ask other questions regarding Kelly.

"In your opinion as a physician, is it possible that Kelly may have survived had she not been left to die that night?"

"Objection Your Honor," said Rudy.

"Overruled, as a matter of professional opinion."

Margie peeked at the coroner, who was sitting rather calmly. "It is possible that she may have survived, yes. Although the exact time of the accident is not known, the type of injuries that Kelly sustained did not kill her on impact. It is likely that she was alive for up to an hour before her death."

Margie pursed her lips together, trying her hardest not to cry. She stole a glance at Morgan, who was sitting, facing forward and stony-faced. Her skin was pale, and her lips were almost white.

Margie wished that she was closer to her so that she could hold her hand, or at least reach out and touch her in some way.

Thankfully, the defense chose not to question the coroner, and he was dismissed along with the graphic pictures.

Next, a car expert was called up to identify the car and bumper. The car was easy enough – there was a grainy video of Andrea driving down the road that night in the 1963 Corvette Stingray. The expert identified the car, and the jury was left to decide for themselves if the driver had a resemblance to Andrea.

After that, the expert described the bumper that was found as well as the tire marks at the scene of the accident. Margie didn't have to be convinced that it was, in fact, a 1963 Corvette Stingray that caused the accident, but she felt that the witness explained everything quite thoroughly for the jury.

This time, however, the defense decided to ask a few questions to poke holes in the argument about the car.

"Isn't it possible," asked Rudy, "that a 1963 Corvette Stingray drove down the road that night, hit its brakes, and drove on, bumper intact, completely *unrelated* to Kelly Allen's accident?"

"I suppose."

"Are there any distinguishing markings on the bumper that guarantee with one hundred perfect certainty that the bumper found at the scene of the accident was in fact from Brock's 1963 Corvette Stingray?"

"Well, upon examining the bumper, I determined that it was in fact the bumper from a 1963 Corvette Stingray."

"Is it possible that another car used the bumper from a Stingray – perhaps as repair work? Or as an upgrade?"

The witness sighed. "That's always possible, of course. But it would be very unusual."

"Were you ever able to examine the car from which this bumper supposedly came?"

The witness shook his head. "No, I was not."

"That's right. Because that car is nowhere to be found."

Margie gritted her teeth. Of course the car was nowhere to be found! Brock dumped it as soon as he realized that Andrea used it to kill Kelly!

But since they didn't have the car, they couldn't prove anything. All Rudy had to do was plant a seed of doubt in the jury's mind and then...well, then they might decide that Andrea wasn't guilty after all.

Margie sat fuming, unable to focus on the rest of the man's testimony.

After that, the prosecution summoned Brock's mechanic to the stand.

"Here I have phone records on the night of Kelly Allen's death showing that Brock called your cell phone *four* times – once at 8:31, then at 8:34, again at 9:14, and finally just before midnight."

He handed the sheet of paper to the jury to examine.

"Do you remember what you were talking about with Brock that evening?"

"I don't remember," he said. "I often do work for Brock – he has a lot of cars. But I don't remember the specifics of that conversation."

"I would also like to introduce a complaint filed against Brock that same evening, when he was arrested for driving under the influence and interestingly, he was driving *your* car. Why would that be?"

"Objection," said Rudy.

"Sustained."

Darn it. Hank said it would be really difficult to introduce any evidence about Brock acting suspiciously that night, mainly because his case of drunk driving was beaten in court.

"If you are familiar with Brock's cars, do you recall ever working on his 1963 Corvette Stingray? I have records showing that he bought and registered the car seven years ago and in fact, was the only owner of a 1963 Corvette Stingray on any of the San Juan Islands."

He shook his head. "I've worked on a lot of his cars, but I don't remember that one in particular."

"Really? This is a classic." Leo held up a picture he had of the Corvette. "You *really* don't remember?"

"I don't remember."

"Did you ever work on this car when it sustained a lot of damage, anything that would make you suspicious that perhaps the car was involved in an accident?"

He cleared his throat. "I do not recall anything like that, no."

Baloney! How was he allowed to lie like that and say that he just didn't remember!

Margie looked at Morgan again, who was still sitting stiff and frozen, fixated on the scene in front of them.

The defense took the opportunity to question the mechanic and ask him softball questions like, "Would you say that Brock is a nice guy to work for?"

It basically gave an opportunity to frame Brock as a great guy and boyfriend, not someone who would ever be involved in the cover-up of a brutal crime.

Well, that was all fine, because Margie knew that Brock was up to testify next. And no jury would ever be able to find that man sympathetic.

Chapter 13

Morgan was grateful when the mechanic finally got off of the stand. Initially, part of her hoped that he would be honest and tell the truth about what he knew from that night.

But as soon as he got up there and started saying how he couldn't remember anything, Morgan knew it was pointless. What was even worse was that the defense used him as a character witness for Brock, claiming that he was this fun car enthusiast and could never participate in murder.

It couldn't be any further from the truth. The only good thing about Brock having so many cars was that he completely forgot that Luke had borrowed one of his cars to drive Andrea off of the island after she confessed to him.

It was a month before he came looking for that car, and Luke hilariously insisted that he misplaced the keys or that it had run out of gas, and then that it had run out of oil.

Finally, Brock hired a tow truck and took the car back by force. It was impressive, though, how long Luke kept the ruse going. He partially did it because he liked the car, but mostly he did it to amuse Morgan.

It worked.

She took a peek at him, seated at her left. He was still staring straight ahead, his expression neutral. She felt like she could fall to pieces at any moment, and very much appreciated his stoic English demeanor.

Every attempt that Brock made at intimidating him as a witness failed. He threatened to take them to court for defamation, and even filed a few lawsuits. Luke got them all dismissed with the help of an attorney friend, and never betrayed any sort of worry about it.

"If I'm about to be hauled off to jail," he'd said, "you'll just have to move to London with me. We'll restart the business, and have quite a lot of fun."

Having Luke and her dad at her side made the trial at least bearable. The worst part were the pictures of her mom.

She tried not to look, but at one point she saw the screen and instantly regretted it. That image would be seared into her mind for the rest of her life, she was sure of it.

But that wasn't how she wanted to remember her mom. Her mom was more than a body on a cold metal table. And if the jury had any sense, they wouldn't let that be the end of her story.

Morgan memorized the order of the witnesses, which Leo generously explained to her and discussed his style of telling the story of a crime.

Next up was Brock.

Leo warned her ahead of time that Brock would very likely refuse to say anything on the stand, but even his refusals would say something to the jury.

Once he was sworn in, Leo began.

"Mr. Brock Hunter, what is your relationship to the defendant?"

"She's my girlfriend."

"And on the night of the accident, were you two together?"

He leaned forward to get closer to the microphone. "On the advice of counsel, I respectfully decline to answer and assert my Fifth Amendment privilege."

"That's okay, Mr. Hunter. Because here I have phone records on the night of the accident which show that you had even more calls to Andrea than you did to your mechanic. It shows here that Andrea, our defendant, called you *fifteen* times on the evening of the accident – with all but one of those calls being after 8 PM."

Leo passed this paper to the jury to examine.

"What were you guys talking about that night?"

Brock leaned forward, again pleading the Fifth. Morgan turned to watch the faces of the jurors as he went through his spiel again.

Juror number two was focused on the phone records. Juror one was sitting, cross armed, and the rest had unreadable expressions, except for juror seven, Morgan's favorite, who she nicknamed "Sweet Grandma." She sat there with her arms crossed and a scowl on her face. Clearly she did not approve of Brock's refusal to cooperate.

"I believe, Mr. Hunter, that you were arrested that evening under the suspicion of driving under the influence. Is that correct?"

Brock looked annoyed, and leaned forward again. "Please let the record state that I was found not guilty of this accusation."

Leo nodded. "Okay Mr. Hunter."

He went on to show the video of Andrea driving the Corvette – which Brock refused to comment on – and asked several more questions: had he and Andrea been fighting that evening? What happened to his 1963 Corvette Stingray? Did Andrea tell him that she'd been involved in an accident that evening?

He refused to answer all of the questions.

When Leo finally gave up, Morgan again studied the jury. A few were taking notes; that was probably good. That meant that they were at least paying attention.

Now it was Rudy's turn to cross examine.

"Mr. Hunter, how long have you and Ms. Collins been together?"

"Three years."

"And in your years with her, has she ever betrayed even the slightest tendencies toward violence?"

"No, absolutely not. She is a kind, gentle person."

"On the evening of the accident, what were the two of you doing?"

"We were enjoying a movie at my house. And while we did get into a little argument, it was nothing unusual for a couple. I can't even remember what it was about."

"Of course not, it's normal for couples to bicker. At any point in that argument, did you witness Andrea running over the victim, Kelly Allen?"

"Absolutely not."

Morgan had to force herself not to snort. What kind of a question was that?

"And is there any way that she could have left your house, driven into Friday Harbor, struck Kelly Allen, and returned without you knowing?"

"No, we were together all night."

"Thank you Mr. Hunter, that is all."

He smiled, stood up, and walked back to his seat. He was sitting with a large group of people, who Morgan assumed must be Andrea's parents or friends. They came all dressed in black as though they were going to a funeral. Morgan tried not to resent every single one of them, but it was hard.

Luke was then called to testify. Morgan squeezed his hand before he stood up, and he winked at her.

If only Leo had found a way to get Andrea's confession to Luke admitted into evidence. But no – it was impossible. It couldn't even be mentioned at trial.

Hopefully Luke could be convincing on his own. As he was sworn in, Morgan said a silent prayer that he wouldn't try to crack any jokes.

"Mr. Pierce, can you please explain your relationship with Brock Hunter?"

Luke nodded. "Brock is my uncle. I spent a few months living with him when I first moved to San Juan Island."

"And was that before or after Kelly Allen's accident?"

"Oh, several months afterward."

"Very good. And had you ever met Andrea in the months that you were living with Brock?"

"No, not in person. Occasionally I would see her on a video chat, but Brock often had many other lady visitors, if you know what I mean."

"Can you please explain."

"Oh right, sorry." Luke cleared his throat. "My Uncle Brock had intimate relations with many women, but I never saw Andrea at the house."

"Objection," said Rudy. "Relevance, Your Honor?"

"Counsel, if you have a point, please make it."

Leo nodded. "Of course Your Honor. So despite Andrea and Brock claiming to be a happy couple, how did you see their relationship?"

"Well, my uncle did an awful lot of sneaking around behind her back. The first time that I met Andrea in person it became obvious why my uncle had been hiding her."

"What do you mean, hiding her?"

"Oh, sorry. He avoided bringing her onto the island. I thought it was strange that they'd been dating so long and that she had *never* visited. The first time that she came to the island, in my knowledge, she made several allusions to the fact that she had not wanted to return."

"What sort of allusions?"

"She specifically said that she did not feel safe driving on the island."

"Is that all that she said?"

Luke nodded. "At the time, yes. But the way that she said it didn't sit right with me. I became aware of Kelly Allen's case and the fact that there was a 1963 Corvette Stingray believed to be involved in the accident. I became suspicious that Andrea and my uncle had been involved in it."

"So what did you do with that knowledge?"

"I wanted to get her to tell me what happened. So I went to my uncle's house and told her that the local police knew that she caused the accident."

"And how did Brock and Andrea react to this news?"

"Andrea panicked, and Brock became very angry. But I told them that I was able to smuggle Andrea off of the island and into Canada so that she wouldn't have to face any consequences for her actions."

"And Andrea agreed to this plan? For you to smuggle her across the border?"

Luke nodded. "She did. And my uncle loaned me a car, and while I was driving her, she confessed the crime to me."

"What did she say?"

"She said that she and my Uncle Brock had been drinking that night and got into an argument. Apparently, she became aware of some of the other women that my uncle was involved with. To get back at him, she took the Corvette from his garage and drove into Friday Harbor. She said that Kelly Allen was in the street when she struck her with the car. She blamed Kelly for being in the street, and told me that she left her at the scene."

"And that was why she agreed to flee the island with you? Because she thought she'd been caught?"

"Yes. She knew exactly what she had done and that it was wrong, and she was afraid that the police had figured it out."

"What happened after she confessed this to you?"

"The police took her into custody."

"Thank you Luke."

"Would the defense like to cross?" asked the judge.

"Yes Your Honor." Rudy stood up, slowly buttoning his jacket and taking his time to get closer to Luke.

"Mr. Pierce, is it true that you are involved in a romantic relationship with Morgan Allen, the victim's daughter?"

"Yes."

"So when you say you became aware of this crime, was it from your girlfriend?"

Luke frowned. "No. I heard about it from my friend Matthew."

"And who is Matthew?"

Luke cleared his throat. "He's a sheriff's deputy here on San Juan Island."

"So you just happened to start dating Morgan Allen, who was likely very upset about the death of her mother. And you *happened* to piece together who did it, and you somehow managed to get a confession from Andrea?"

"Well – no, it wasn't like that exactly."

"So you *didn't* get her confession?"

Morgan could see that Luke was gritting his teeth. "To be perfectly clear, I absolutely got a confession from her and she wanted my help in escaping before the police found her."

"So this 'confession,' and a blurry video of a blonde woman driving a Corvette somehow prove that Andrea is guilty?"

"Yes."

"And the fact that *you* put all of this together – that's very convenient in winning over your new girlfriend, don't you think?"

"Objection, badgering the witness."

"Sustained."

Rudy started talking again. "Who's to say that you didn't make up this entire story to get back at your uncle, who refused to give you the money and cars that you thought you deserved?"

"My only intention in going to see Andrea and Uncle Brock that day was to see if she was foolish enough to tell me everything she'd done. And she was."

"Sure, according to you. How can we possibly know that you didn't just offer to give her a ride and then handed her over to the police?"

"Because I didn't. She confessed. She even packed a bag so she could make her escape."

"Is it not true, then, after you concocted this story you kept your uncle's car in order to impress your girlfriend, Morgan Allen?"

"No," Luke said, leaning slightly forward. "He gave me that car willingly, to help her escape. And later, he got it back."

Rudy smiled. "Thank you Mr. Pierce."

Luke was dismissed and Leo announced that the prosecution was resting their case. The judge asked the defense to call their first witness.

Rudy stood. "Your Honor, after conferring with my client, I respectfully request a recess for the rest of today."

Judge Gore frowned. "All right. In that case, court is adjourned for today. We will resume tomorrow."

Morgan's eyes darted around, trying to make sense of why court was ending so early. She didn't know what it all meant, so she decided to talk to Leo and get his take.

Chapter 14

The timing of the end of the trial's first day came as a surprise to Tiffany, but she wasn't entirely disappointed that it was over early.

She'd felt tense the entire time and didn't know what to think. At first, she thought the prosecution was doing well in painting a picture of Andrea's guilt; but she had to admit that the defense attorney did make Luke's testimony questionable. It might've been the best evidence that they had, but he tried to make Luke look like a bitter relative.

Morgan, Ronny, and Luke all met with the prosecutor in a private room before rejoining the group back at Margie's house.

Tiffany tried not to be too pushy, but once Morgan was inside, she couldn't help it. "So what did Leo say?"

"He thinks we still have a pretty strong case. And that if Andrea were smart, she'd be begging for a plea deal admitting to her guilt."

"But I'm guessing she's not going to do that?"

Morgan shook her head. "We don't know, but it doesn't seem like it."

Ronny sighed. "There must be a reason that the defense asked for a recess, though. Leo said that Andrea looked pretty agitated as the day went on, and he wonders if she's demanding to testify."

"Why though? Then she can be cross-examined by the prosecution, right?" asked Jade. "What do you think she'd do?

I mean – if she were up on the stand? Do you really think she would lie?"

"Ha! Of *course* she would lie!" said Morgan. "I think she would do anything to save herself. I think that's exactly why her attorney doesn't want to put her up on the stand."

Luke took a seat, letting out a huff. "I can't believe I let him get to me like that."

"Don't take it too hard," said Chief Hank. "You had to answer his questions, and he had to make it look like you were unreliable."

"But I'm *not* unreliable! Everything I said was true. If only the jury could actually hear the recording of Andrea's confession. They would definitely convict her, there was such glee in her voice. She thought it was *funny,* what she'd done."

Morgan sat down next to him. "I know. But the defense made sure that we couldn't get that into evidence."

"Don't despair yet," Ronny said, taking a seat next to her.

"Is anyone up for some lunch? Or, uh, dinner plans?" asked Chief Hank. "Margie has been making food all week."

"My kitchen," she said, "is always open."

Morgan stood up. "Thanks Margie. But I think my dad and I are going to get something in town and just...talk things over. If that's okay?"

"Of course it is!" she said. "We'll be here when you need us, okay?"

She nodded. "Thanks guys. Are you ready to go, Dad?"

"Sure. Thank you all for coming today – it really does mean a lot to us both."

"Of course," said Chief Hank. "Please let me know if there's anything that I can do."

He smiled. "Thank you."

After they left, Tiffany decided that she would leave, too. She hadn't had a chance yet to update Jade on her talks with Sidney, and she was hoping to have some time to dig around the internet to see if she could find anything else suspicious.

On their way home, she told Jade all about what Sidney had found.

"But that doesn't really mean anything, though," said Jade. "Does it? Maybe someone saw the parks department would get a bunch of money and they just wanted to raise their own money to fight new projects."

"Well," Tiffany said with a scoff, "What about that guy who wants to sell off the killer whales?"

"That's just terrible," Jade said, shaking her head. "The whales that live here are actually considered an endangered species! There are less than a hundred whales and only like thirty of them are still at reproductive age. I mean, come on! How evil can you get?"

"I know. I'm not sure how it relates to the parks budget – or if it even relates at all. But I have a feeling that it does."

"I really appreciate you spending so much time on this Tiffany," said Jade. "And I know that you don't want his help, but maybe Dad would actually know something?"

Tiffany groaned. "I mean, I'll talk to him, for you, but I'm going to try to do it on my own first. I have Sidney's help, and so far he's been very...impressive."

Jade turned toward her. "Impressive? What does that mean?"

Oh dear, she'd said too much. "You know, he's just...very dedicated. And serious – you know how serious he is."

"Oh I know," Jade said. "I hope he hasn't been mean to you."

"Not at all. He's been really nice, actually. He's much different than I thought he was." She paused. "He's not like Eric, you know. Don't get me wrong – I like Eric a lot. But Sidney never had anything handed to him. And it shows."

"If I didn't know any better, I'd think that you kind of admire him?" Jade said with a little smile.

"I'd say that I think I kind of do?" said Tiffany. "Talk about the surprise of the decade."

When they got home, Tiffany locked herself away in her bedroom and spent hours pouring over donation records and fundraising information. She didn't find anything substantial.

Her next move was to look at some of the parks department employees. It was easy enough to find information about them – their names and positions, at least. She then took a page out of the single woman playbook and spent some time stalking them online.

She was able to see Facebook profiles for some of the higher ups in the parks department. Unfortunately, nothing jumped out at her or screamed fraud.

After hours of searching, she had the urge to reach out to Sidney to see if he'd found anything. She hesitated, though. She didn't want Sidney to think she was some kind of an amateur who couldn't do anything useful.

But on the other hand, he knew that she was an amateur. He now knew her whole history. Despite all of that, he still wanted to keep working with her – and with Jade. Why was he so committed to this project?

Oh yeah. Because Eric was committed to it, and he needed to show the great Uncle Dan that he could be successful.

But where was Eric during all of this? Tiffany knew that Jade was still talking with him and discussing plans, but from where she was standing, it seemed like Sidney was working much harder toward the success of this project than Eric was.

That might not be true though – she was letting her own bias seep through again. Now that she knew more about Sidney, she really did admire him.

Despite having an extremely difficult upbringing where he had to grow up way too fast, he didn't seem to hang onto any bitterness.

Quite the contrary – he was more than willing to offer his time, dedication, and expertise in helping his cousin succeed. It seemed almost unfair, though. Eric had every opportunity at his disposal.

Sidney had to prove his worth, and he spent all of his time taking care of everyone else. First it was his dad and his little brother, now it was Eric and Rachel. Where did he get the energy?

They'd had such a lovely time together on the boat...

And while they spent time talking about their theories related to the grant funding, they also talked a lot about their families. Tiffany even told him about her old job and relation-ship with Malcolm, and Sidney listened intently with those beautiful, dark eyes focused on her.

It was really an enchanting evening. He was lovely to talk to, and she realized that she would've been just as happy talking to him on that little dinghy as she was on the yacht.

Did he treat *all* of his clients to that kind of...luxury? Was that an Uncle Dan trick?

Could be. But if she didn't know any better, she'd think that he might...kind of like her.

It was hard to tell, though. She had a similar back-and-forth with Malcolm at her old job. They were always teasing each other, always in a friendly competition.

More than once, Tiffany felt like maybe, one day, she and Malcolm would become more than friends. But she didn't want to jeopardize her career by making the first move, and he probably didn't either. So nothing ever happened.

Now she would never know how he'd felt. It made her heart feel heavy to think of him. She missed him and had so many regrets.

Tiffany sat, staring at her phone. No emails or messages from Sidney.

It was impossible for her to figure out if he liked her unless she said something. It seemed too dangerous to come out and *say* it, though.

She could try hinting at him, like she wished she'd tried with Malcolm. It could open up a window of opportunity! And he was probably used to getting hit on by women all the time – if he didn't like her, he'd ignore it.

Or, there was a chance that it'd get super awkward.

No. She couldn't think like that. Tiffany wanted one of her values to be honesty, especially with herself. And the truth was, she liked him. A *lot*.

She couldn't remember the last time she'd felt this way about a guy, other than with Malcolm. Sidney reminded her of Malcolm, too – he was all serious until all of a sudden, he opened up.

Was there a way she could figure out how Sidney felt without jeopardizing the project? She didn't want to make him uncomfortable, but at the same time...she only had one life to live, and so much of it had already passed her by.

Whatever. She was just going to go for it.

She smiled to herself and typed out a message. "Hey Sidney, how's it going? I've been trying to think of an excuse to reach out to you all evening. I haven't been able to find anything new about the funding, but still wanted to say hello. So – hello."

She stared at it for a moment. It certainly wasn't her most eloquent message. But there was enough of an out for him – he could say hello back and respond professionally that he hadn't found anything either, and wish her good night. Or...he could pick up on her hint.

She hit send, chucked her phone onto the bed and giggled like a maniac.

That was something she *never* would've done a year ago. Never!

But now? She didn't even think that long about it. Maybe this trial was making her lose her mind.

Her phone dinged and she ran over to it.

He responded!

"Hey Tiffany, that's funny, because I've been looking for an excuse to take you to dinner on Friday, and I couldn't come up with anything either. Are you free?"

"Oh. My. *Gosh*!" She said out loud. "Jade!"

No response. Tiffany walked over to Jade's room and knocked on the door.

"Come in!"

"Hey Sis – I might've done something I shouldn't have done."

Jade looked at her with wide eyes. "What did you do?"

"I kind of...hit on Sidney."

Jade gasped. "What!"

"Yeah," Tiffany nodded. "And I think he hit on me too?"

"Are you serious?"

Tiffany grimaced. Maybe Jade would be upset with her. "Yeah. Look."

She handed over her phone and watched as Jade read the text messages, her hand darting to her mouth.

"I did not expect this at all," Jade said. "From *either* of you!"

"Are you mad? Do you think it's a bad idea? I didn't expect that he would say something like *that*! I just thought I would feel it out and...I don't know!"

Jade handed the phone back, smiling widely. "Well, it looks like you have a date, sister."

"Really? Do you think it's okay? Now I'm second-guessing myself – I never used to mix my business and my personal life, and – "

Jade waved a hand. "Don't worry about that. Do you like him?"

Tiffany smiled. "I do."

Jade shrugged. "Then do it! This project might die anyway, so something good might as well come out of it."

Tiffany felt like squealing. "You're the best. All right, I'll tell him that I'd love to go to dinner."

"Good!"

"Then I'm going to go *right* to bed," said Tiffany. "We have to be in court early again tomorrow, right?"

Jade nodded. "Right. And I can't wait to see what Andrea's lawyers have come up with."

"Me too. Okay, I'm going to send this text and go right to sleep."

Tiffany turned around and headed back to her room; her heart no longer feeling heavy – it felt like it was glowing.

Chapter 15

The judge announced that everyone could be seated, and Morgan was careful to slowly lower herself into the wooden chair. Yesterday during the trial, she sat so still that she tweaked a muscle in her back.

As soon as she'd settled into her seat, she felt the familiar pain of the awkward positioning. She let out a sigh; Morgan knew that everything about this trial would stick in her memory for the rest of her life, including how cold and stiff she felt as she sat, transfixed by what was going on in front of her.

The judge cleared his throat. "Okay everyone, let's try this again. Will the defense please call their first witness?"

Rudy stood. "Thank you, Your Honor. The defense calls Andrea Collins to the stand."

Morgan's stomach dropped and the courtroom erupted in whispers and excitement. Andrea stood slowly, straightening out her dress before making her way to the stand.

Judge Gore asked everyone to be quiet, and by the time Andrea was sworn in, it was again silent in the courtroom.

"Andrea. We've heard a lot about your relationship with Brock from everybody else, but not from you. Tell me, how long were you two together?"

She took a deep breath and nodded. "We were together for three years."

"Did Brock have other relationships on the side?"

She nodded again. "Yes sir. I was very devoted to Brock, but he was not as devoted to me."

Rudy sighed. "I see. And on the night of Kelly Allen's death, were you with Brock?"

"Yes."

"What were you doing?"

"We were having a nice evening, at first. We went to dinner and walked around town holding hands."

Rudy smiled. "Was Brock a good boyfriend?"

"I thought so at the time..." She paused, letting her voice trail off.

Clearly a talented actress.

She quietly cleared her throat. "But he had a temper, and *such* a hold over me. There were other women – I knew about them, and we would fight about it, and he would always promise that it was the last time."

"That sounds hard. Did you love him?"

"Very much. My love for him was blind."

Rudy walked around, slowly circling in front of the jury. "Can you tell me what happened the rest of that evening?"

"We went back to his house and he started to drink alcohol. Heavily. He gets so cruel when he drinks, and he started to tell me about the other women that he was seeing and how he didn't need me."

"That sounds awful. Is this the argument that he claims not to remember?"

"Yes."

"Do you think he does remember?"

"I'm not surprised he doesn't remember with how much he was drinking," Andrea said.

Morgan rolled her eyes. When Andrea confessed the crime to Luke, she made it clear that she'd *also* had a lot to drink and how normal that was for both of them.

"I told him that I wasn't going to take it anymore and I was leaving."

"And how did you leave?"

"I tried to walk out, but he struck me. In the face!"

There was more murmuring in the courtroom and the judge again asked for silence.

Rudy continued. "And then what happened?"

Andrea whimpered.

"It's okay, you can tell us," Rudy added, reassuringly.

Morgan shot a look at the jury – they couldn't believe this nonsense, could they? What was this act that she was putting on?

She took a deep breath and spoke again. "I was so afraid. I ran outside and planned to lock myself in the car I found out front. He came outside and was so wild that I was frightened."

"What car was that?"

"It was the Corvette. The Stingray."

"So what did you do?"

"The keys were already in there so I tried to escape. I drove away, but he came after me in another car, and he caught up with me in town."

"And what did he do then?"

"He pulled his car in front of me and I had to stop. Then he got in and told me that he would kill me if I didn't start listening to him."

Rudy paused for a moment and smiled warmly at her. "You're doing great. What happened after that?"

Andrea let out a big sigh. "He got into the driver's seat of the Corvette. He was so angry and driving so erratically...just barreling through town. And then, all of a sudden, I heard a scream and a thump. He'd hit Kelly Allen with the car."

There was a gasp in the courtroom; someone shouted something in the back.

The judge hit his gavel. "If anyone else has an outburst, you will be removed."

The clamor died down. Morgan sat frozen, her stare fixed on Andrea. She couldn't believe what she was hearing.

"What happened after Brock hit her?" Rudy asked.

"I begged him to stop and help her, but he just struck me again." Andrea began to cry quiet, jerking tears. "I was so afraid of him and afraid to tell the truth."

"Thank you, Andrea," Rudy said, taking a seat. "No more questions."

Morgan looked at Leo, who was fiercely writing notes down on a sheet of paper.

"Would the prosecution like to cross-examine the witness?" asked the judge.

Leo stood up. "Your Honor, I would like to ask for an emergency recess in light of this new information."

"We can't end early *every* day," the judge said with a sigh. "However, considering the unexpected developments...your request for an emergency recess is granted."

The gallery again erupted around Morgan. She could hear Chief explaining why he thought Leo didn't try to cross-examine Andrea – he reasoned that Leo wasn't prepared because her testimony had shocked everyone.

Morgan didn't want to get into a discussion about it just yet; she kept her eyes focused on Andrea.

No one seemed to be paying much attention to her now. She was still sitting on the stand, quiet and doe-eyed – her tears nowhere to be seen.

Chapter 16

"Let's hope he's in a good mood today," said Eric.

Sidney looked at his watch. "Well, he should've just had lunch. That'll help our case."

"Excellent thinking, as always, Sid." Eric flashed a smile before opening the door to Dan's office

Sidney followed. His only goal today was to buy more time for Burke Development – and to keep Dan from asking too many unanswerable questions.

"My boys!" Dan said as they walked in, giving Eric a hug.

"Hey Dad!"

"Nice to see you." Sidney smiled and shook Dan's hand. He did seem to be in a good mood, so that was lucky.

"How's it going? How's business?"

Eric clapped his hands together. "Business is good. No – great! I've been making a lot of connections and meeting a lot of great people."

"That's all fine, but how is that island project coming?"

"Really good, Dad. Let me show you some of the plans that we've made up for this place."

Sidney sat back and let Eric do the talking. He was always better at this sort of thing and his enthusiasm could win over almost anyone.

Of course, Dan really wanted him to succeed, so he was much easier on him than he would be on anyone else.

They went through the 3D model and building plans for the park on San Juan. Dan was impressed by the designs, though he worried that they might be a bit too ambitious for a state park.

"What kind of problems have you run into so far?" he asked.

Eric shrugged. "Nothing major. It's been great."

"Well..." Sidney leaned forward. "That's not exactly true. The Washington State Parks Department has run into some funding issues."

Dan crossed his arms. "Hm. Is that going to be a problem?"

Eric opened his mouth to respond and Sidney shot him a look – he didn't want Eric stretching the truth, so it was better if he answered. "Possibly. The county won a grant from the state to build the park, and it looked like the project was a sure thing. But now, with the parks department running out of money, a big chunk of their funding is up in the air."

"But!" Eric interjected, holding up a finger. "They're looking into other sources and are really motivated to get this project off the ground."

"I'll be honest, Eric, I don't like it," Dan said. "It doesn't matter if you've won the bid if there's no money to pay you. What's the plan for how much longer you're going to wait for this?"

Sidney sighed. He knew this was coming. "We haven't set a time limit yet."

"Well, set one," Dan responded, walking back to his desk. "The plans you have here are great, but if you can't do a project this big out of the gate, no one will fault you for it. What about that lead I told you about in Oregon? That glamorous camping place they're trying to build?"

"The glamping site?" Eric made a face. "I don't know about that. It's not really the sort of image we're going for."

"Who cares about your image? It's good work!"

Sidney knew they were getting into a conversation that would make everyone unhappy, so he decided to jump in. "I'm working with them closely on the funding, and I won't hesitate to pull the plug when we need to."

Dan studied him for a moment. "Good. That's what I like to hear. I'm excited for you boys. You get to really do this together. It's something that your dad and I never had, Sidney."

Sidney nodded. "I know. I appreciate the chance, and I promise that we'll figure it out."

He didn't have much more time to meet with them, so Eric quickly summarized a few last key points before it was time to leave.

When they walked out of the office, Eric punched Sidney in the shoulder and said, "Not bad, man! That could've gone much worse."

"Next time, it *will* go much worse," said Sidney. "We have to figure everything out, and soon. Have you or Jade found anything that might work for financing?"

Eric shook his head. "No. I've gone to a couple of organizations that were interested in funding the project, but their grants just aren't big enough for what we want to do."

"Maybe we need to scale back, then?"

"No, we can't! This is a perfect vision – if we change anything, it all falls to pieces."

"I don't know if that's true, but if we can't get the money to do it, it'll definitely fall apart."

Eric shrugged. "Maybe we could have our own fundraiser. I could do that, right?"

Sidney shook his head. "I'm doubtful that you'd be able to raise the kind of money that we need. And that's a huge conflict of interest on your part."

"Well, have you or Tiffany figured out what's going on with the grant? Finding anyone to point fingers at?"

Sidney laughed. "No, not exactly. We found that super PAC, but now I keep running into dead ends."

"Oh, I thought you might've figured something out after you took the boat out on Tuesday."

Sidney turned toward him. "How did you know that I took the boat out?"

Eric smiled. "I like to keep an eye on my partner."

Sidney glared at him until he spoke again.

"All right, that's not exactly true. I needed to ask you a question about the plumbers and I couldn't find you. So, your assistant told me where you were."

"Ah. That makes more sense."

"I thought that since we won the bid we didn't need to impress them anymore?" Eric added with a smile.

"It's always good to keep the lines of communication open," responded Sidney.

"Sure. I believe you."

"Listen Eric – your dad's right. We need to set a limit on this project. I hate to do this, but we have to have something to show for our work, and soon."

"Oh come on man! You can't tell me that you don't trust them."

"It's not that. It's not their fault that they don't have the money, but...they don't have the money. If we're going to run a business, we need to – "

Eric shook his head. "You know, sometimes you sound *just* like my dad. You know that this project is special. And we're partnering with them – we need to have faith."

Sidney sighed. "There's faith and then there's foolishness."

"This is because you don't like Tiffany, isn't it?"

"No, that's not it. I actually...really admire her."

Eric paused. "Oh yeah?"

Sidney decided that he might as well come clean. "I'm taking her to dinner tomorrow."

Eric stopped in his tracks. "Like...on a business dinner?"

"No." He shook his head. "Not a business dinner."

A smile spread across Eric's face. "Sid! I can't believe you!"

"Like I said, it's not that I don't trust them or like them, because I do," Sidney continued. "But we – "

"So you've got the hots for Tiffany and you *still* want to abandon her park!"

"Of course not. And I didn't – I don't have the 'hots' – "

"Uh huh."

Sidney ignored him and kept talking. "The fact is, even *they* understand that we can't go forward with the project if there's no money to do it."

"Then we wait. What if we start on another project and when they're ready, we miss our chance? If – "

"We just need to set a limit. That's all I'm saying, Eric. Think about it, okay?"

He waved a hand, not allowing Sidney to say anything that would ruin his good cheer. "Yeah, fine. When you go on your date, ask Tiffany what's up."

"Maybe I don't want to ruin our evening with business talk," Sidney said with a smile.

Eric laughed. "Fine. Call her today, I don't care. Work your magic, Sidney."

Magic. "All right Eric. I'll see you later."

"See you!"

Sidney went back to his office, fully planning to focus on work, but his mind was preoccupied. Maybe he *would* take Eric's advice and call Tiffany.

He'd been looking for an excuse to talk to her again, and he'd hate to break the news at dinner that Burke Development would soon pursue other projects. He was confident that she wouldn't take it personally, though, and that it wouldn't hurt their relationship.

Ha. Their relationship. He was already thinking in those terms. There wasn't much there yet, but he felt like there would be. Every moment that he spent with her was enthralling, and whenever he wasn't with her, he was distracted by his thoughts of her.

All week he'd been going over their time together in his head – replaying things that she said and the jokes that she made. He remembered different stories that he'd told her and cringed at the memories, wondering if she thought the stories were boring or that he was silly.

But then he would remember how she laughed or how she shot back at him with a clever comment, and the feeling melted away.

Her charm caught him entirely by surprise. He might've missed it totally, even, if she hadn't snapped him out of his self-absorbed trance by calling him out on his own rudeness.

It had been years since he stepped outside of himself and had any...romantic feelings toward someone. And the only other time he'd felt *this* caught up was many, many years ago. He'd met a beautiful, charming, intelligent woman named

Priscilla when he was in college. She was a lot like Tiffany in some ways – she was driven, funny, and beautiful.

At the time, he was young and still battling to get himself and his brother through college. He'd never been in love before, but with the delicate innocence of a first love, he loved her with all of his being. He thought that she felt the same way.

That's what she told him, at least. But once she realized that he was not cut from the same cloth as Eric – when she realized that he had no fortune, and in her eyes, no future – she broke it off.

"I need someone who is as dedicated to success as I am," she'd said.

The phrase was burned into his memory with the fine precision that only rejection can command. It took Sidney years to admit to himself what she'd really meant – she meant that she needed someone who wasn't *quite* as poor as he was.

He ran into Priscilla again just last year. Even though it was more than a decade since they'd last spoken, she seemed unchanged – beautiful, and charming in that easy, elegant way. But he could now more clearly see the ruthlessness in her manner, especially as she asked him question after question about his role at Burke Industries.

All of a sudden he was interesting again, but as she asked about projects and materials, he knew what the real question was, dancing behind the renewed light in her eyes: "How much?"

Sidney was surprised that he had no urge to answer that question for her; she didn't have the hold on him that she once did. He was a different person now, and was able to walk away at the end of the night with his head held high. He politely answered the emails and texts she sent after their meeting, but made no offer of friendship. Eventually, she faded back into history.

It took him a long time to get to that point, though, where he was able to move on. He took the rejection and betrayal to heart.

After so many years of never falling in love again, he wondered if he honestly was even cut out for it – perhaps the one, exceptionally painful instance was enough.

But then, out of nowhere, came Tiffany.

She was different, he could just feel it. Plus, he was older and wiser. He felt like it was a risk, yes – but a calculated one. One he was willing to take.

He typed out a text message. "How's the trial going? Met with Uncle Dan and Eric today – I'll have to tell you about it."

She answered a few minutes later. "The trial is wild. Things took an unexpected turn. I hope nothing bad from your uncle?"

Maybe a text message wasn't the best way to break the news. He spent a few minutes forming a response.

"He's okay for now, but our time is running low. I'll tell you more tomorrow."

She sent back a smiley face and said "looking forward to it."

He smiled to himself. He was looking forward to seeing her, too.

In fact, he couldn't stop thinking about it. He'd made a reservation at one of his favorite restaurants north of the city. He'd already spent an hour studying the menu to make sure he had something good to recommend to her.

As much as he liked to tell himself that he was making a rational decision to go out with her, he knew the truth – he was powerless against her charms.

Hopefully, she wouldn't abuse that power.

Chapter 17

By Friday morning, even Tiffany's nerves were starting to fray. She'd spent most of the previous evening trying to reassure Morgan that Leo knew what he was doing and that the jury wasn't going to fall for Andrea's theatrics.

But privately, Tiffany wasn't so sure. Andrea had thrown a real curveball and the prosecution didn't have much time to react.

Court resumed with the judge reminding everyone that outbursts would not be tolerated in his courtroom. He then prompted the prosecution to present any evidence that they had.

Leo looked ready. "We would like to call Brock Hunter to the stand."

Yikes.

Tiffany hoped that this wouldn't devolve into a game of he said, she said. Neither one of them were particularly likable, but Brock was even more detestable than Andrea, somehow.

He was sworn in and took his seat.

"Mr. Hunter – yesterday we got to hear Andrea's recollection of the night that Kelly Allen died. I understand that you would now like to give us your side of the story?"

"I would."

"First off, I'm sure the jury is wondering – why did you decide to come forward now?"

"I was trying to protect Andrea, but I can't stand for her perpetuating these scandalous falsehoods."

Tiffany turned and made a face at Jade, mouthing "scandalous falsehoods?" Jade rolled her eyes.

"So, what really happened that night?" asked Leo.

"Andrea and I did get into a fight, that much is true. But I *never* touched her. She took the Corvette to get back at me, and *she* hit Kelly Allen with the car."

"Okay Mr. Hunter. And what evidence do you have of this?"

"I have the car. And I have her cell phone from that night, which she left behind in the car."

"Why did she leave it behind?"

"She wanted me to destroy it. Along with the car."

Tiffany's jaw dropped and there was murmuring all around her.

"Your Honor, we'd like to introduce into evidence this cell phone, along with this transcript of messages between the defendant, Andrea Collins, and Mr. Brock Hunter, from the night of Kelly's death."

A picture of the car went up onto the courtroom screens, showing damage to the front hood.

Leo held up a cell phone in one hand and a pile of papers in the other.

"Ladies and gentlemen of the jury, I have written transcripts from this phone for each of you." He handed out the stacks of paper. "Please allow me to read the text messages that Andrea sent to Mr. Hunter on the evening of Kelly Allen's death. Starting at 7:47 PM Andrea writes, 'You're going to be sorry that you ever met me.' What did that mean to you, Mr. Hunter?"

"She was angry and jealous. She said that after she'd taken the car, so I assumed she was going to damage it in some way."

Leo clicked to a new picture on the screen – this one was a selfie of Andrea in the car, smiling. Tiffany had to bite her lip not to laugh. Why did people take selfies of themselves doing the *dumbest* things?

"A minute later, she sent you this picture of herself in the Corvette?"

"That's correct."

"Ladies and gentleman of the jury, you can read along with me here – twelve minutes later, Andrea sent a message pleading with Mr. Hunter to pick up the phone because something bad had happened. The next four messages are her begging for Mr. Hunter to answer her phone calls, with her final message saying, 'This is serious, I think I just killed somebody.'"

Tiffany watched the jurors' faces as they leafed through the papers – they looked quite engaged now.

"When did you make contact with Andrea again?"

"It was after that message," Brock said, nodding. "I thought she was kidding, but I finally called her and she told me that she had hit someone with the car. She was crying and saying that she didn't know what to do. She begged for my help."

"And what did you do?"

"I told her to drive back to the house and we would take care of it."

"What did you mean by 'take care?' "

Brock sighed. "The plan was to scrap the car – rip it to pieces so that no one could find it again. But...I had a hard time doing that. It was in mint condition, and there wasn't that much damage to it. Then, I decided to hold onto the cell phone in case she ever decided to change her story."

"So to be clear, it was Andrea, and not you, who was driving the car that struck Kelly Allen?"

"That's correct. And I'm not going to protect her anymore."

"Thank you Mr. Hunter. I have no more questions."

Tiffany shot a look at Rudy. He was sitting there, just shaking his head.

Judge Gore spoke. "Defense, do you want to cross?"

Rudy straightened when he answered. "No Your Honor."

"Very well. Does the prosecution have any more witnesses?"

"No Your Honor."

Judge Gore nodded. "Defense, are you ready to present your closing argument?"

Rudy stood up. "Yes, Your Honor."

Tiffany leaned forward slightly so she could get a look at Morgan and Ronny. Morgan was leaning over, whispering something in her dad's ear. Tiffany caught her eye and winked. Morgan smiled broadly and winked back. Clearly, Brock's testimony had raised her spirits.

"Ladies and gentlemen of the jury, what you have before you are two very different accounts of one very tragic evening. Only days ago, Brock Hunter stood before us and refused to say anything about the night in question. And now he's suddenly come into possession of all of this evidence?"

Rudy paused, letting out a sigh. "I am not here to try Brock Hunter on this crime, but it's quite convenient that he suddenly found the car in question and can point the finger back at my client. Once again, Andrea is a victim of his abuse. And like so many women in this country who suffer at the hands of cruel men, Andrea was afraid to tell the truth."

Tiffany looked at the jurors. They were all watching Rudy carefully, betraying nothing on their faces.

"What we're asking you today is to look deep into your hearts, to look at the evidence presented here and determine, *truly* determine, that there is absolutely *no doubt* in your mind that Andrea committed this crime. That there is no doubt that Brock, who had her living in fear, found a way to pin this terrible act on her.

"The prosecution was supposed to prove to us, without a reasonable doubt, that Andrea committed this crime. And what did they give us?"

He stood for a moment, as though he was waiting for them to answer.

"Nothing." He shook his head. "They gave us nothing. They showed us a video of Andrea driving the car. Which was true – she admitted to driving the car. But only to get away from her abuser.

"Then, the prosecution called their star witness, her abuser, Brock Hunter. And he refused to say anything! Yet when Andrea told her story – the truth, mind you – of how he'd victimized her and forced her to stay quiet – *then* he wanted to talk. And what did he have?

"Suddenly he has the car. He just found it! He just found it out of nowhere. And he's got these text messages?"

Rudy held up the stack of papers before dropping them onto the table. "Who knows if he fabricated all of this? I didn't have time to look at it. My experts didn't have time to look at it. It's a lot of evidence for an innocent person to have."

He paused again, stepping closer to the jury. "But that is why you are all here today. You are here to decide the truth. And if there is *any* chance that someone else was behind the wheel of that car, then you would condemn the wrong person and only add to this horrible tragedy.

"If you're not able to look into the depths of your conscience to be certain that the right person has been accused, we ask that you return with a verdict of not guilty."

Tiffany shifted in her seat. So that was why this guy cost so much money. Not for Andrea, of course – but for her dad, who sat sour-faced in the back.

Leo got up to make his closing argument. "The defense will argue that you cannot possibly have enough evidence to know who killed Kelly Allen that night. They'd have you believe that Brock Hunter is a liar.

"But no – he was just a man trying to protect the woman that he loves. When it came to it, though, he's chosen to do the right thing and come clean. There is no way that in the short time since we all met yesterday that Brock could have fabricated this evidence – the car, the text messages, even the picture that Andrea took of herself driving that night.

"He showed us what happened that evening with Andrea's *own* words – her own messages and frantic calls confessing to what she had done, and begging him to help her get out of trouble. But who was there for Kelly Allen when she was in trouble?"

Leo stopped to look at each and every one of the jurors. "No one. Because Andrea, in her never ending selfishness, cared only about one thing – herself. She left Kelly to die, and now wants you to believe some fable that *she* is actually the victim in all of this.

"Ladies and gentlemen, we ask you for a guilty verdict to bring Andrea to justice at last."

Judge Gore thanked him and then began to address the jury – explaining the charges, what their duty was as jurors, and what reasonable doubt meant.

It was a long spiel that took almost a full hour; once he was through it, the jury was sent away to conduct their deliberations.

Most of the spectators in the courtroom had already left by that time. Leo came over to chat with them and explained that the deliberations sometimes reached a verdict right away, but considering the big revelations that had come so late in the trial, he expected that this might take a bit longer.

"What should we do?" asked Margie. "Should we wait here? Or wait at home? I'm not sure what's better."

"I recommend that you go home and try to relax," said Leo. "I'll call you the second we know that the jury will deliver their verdict."

"I think I'll stay here," Morgan said quietly. "You guys are free to go."

"Well *that's* not happening," said Tiffany. "We'll all stay. I'll go and get some food for everyone."

Tiffany took down their orders and came back forty minutes later with food, as promised. After eating, they tried to kill time as they waited, chatting and telling stories.

Finally, when five o'clock struck, it was announced that the jury would reconvene on Monday to continue deliberations.

Morgan groaned. "I don't know how I'm going to make it to Monday."

Ronny put his arm around her. "The same way we got through the rest of this nightmare. One day at a time."

They headed back to Margie and Hank's house and passed the time with playing board games. There were plans for a light dinner, and Tiffany felt guilty leaving the group to go out with Sidney.

"Maybe I'll just postpone it to next week," she said.

Jade shook her head. "Oh come on, don't do that! Morgan, would you be upset if Tiffany went on a date with Sidney tonight?"

"What's this?" Morgan asked. "Are you kidding me? You have a date and you didn't even tell me!"

"Well, you've been a little busy with more important things," said Tiffany.

"This is the kind of news I need to hear. You *definitely* need to go."

Just then, Tiffany's phone rang. She didn't recognize the number, but thought that perhaps Sidney was calling from a work site or something?

"Excuse me," she said, stepping away. "Hello?"

"Hi, Tiffany?"

She frowned; Tiffany didn't recognize the voice. "Yes?"

A sob erupted from the other end of the phone.

Oh dear. "Hello? Are you there?"

"Tiffany, I'm sorry. It's Rachel, I don't know if you remember me."

"Of course I do – what's wrong Rachel?"

"I'm in trouble. And I didn't know who to call."

Tiffany let out a sigh. "What happened? Do you need me to call Sidney?"

"No! Please don't – " She started crying again. "Never mind – I'm just going to – "

"Okay, I won't call him. What's the matter, where are you?"

"I'm on Orcas Island." Another sob. "At some stupid hotel."

"Send me the address. I'll be there soon."

Tiffany pulled Jade aside and told her about the call she'd just received, and Jade quickly offered her the keys to her car.

"Do you want me to come with you?" asked Jade.

Tiffany shook her head. "No – it's okay. I'll be fine. I just need to find out what kind of trouble she's gotten herself into this time."

Jade nodded. "Good luck."

Tiffany made it just in time to catch the inter-island ferry to Orcas Island. If she focused, she *might* have enough time to get to the mainland to meet Sidney. Although...she wasn't sure where Rachel needed to go.

No time to think about it now. She plugged the hotel address into her phone's GPS so she could get there straight off of the ferry.

When she got to the hotel, she dialed Rachel's number again.

"Hey! I'm here, where are you?"

"Oh, I think I see you."

Tiffany watched as a far-off figure stood up from a bench on the side of the hotel. It was definitely Rachel – once again in a short and tight dress, but this time with mascara staining her cheeks.

Tiffany sighed. What had she gotten herself into?

She got out of the car and waved at her; Rachel ran over as best as she could in her stiletto heels.

Once inside, Tiffany started asking questions. "All right Rachel – what's going on?"

"I'm really sorry, I didn't have anyone else that I could call."

"What happened? Are you okay?"

She nodded, taking a deep breath. "I'm such an idiot. You can't tell Sidney – if he finds out, he's not going to let me start college in the fall."

"Rachel," Tiffany said gently, "Sidney wants the best for you. You should be honest with him."

Rachel scoffed. "Yeah right, he just wants to control me."

Okay, so *that* technique wasn't going to work.

Tiffany cleared her throat. "Listen, it's hard for him to understand what it's like to be a young woman. But he just wants you to be safe. You don't have to tell me what happened, but I just want you to know that if you are in some kind of trouble, I can help."

Rachel shook her head. "I'm not in trouble. I don't think. Do you promise that you won't tell him?"

Tiffany bit her lip. Maybe she could convince Rachel to tell him eventually – and it'd be better if she knew the severity of the problem now. "I promise."

"Okay. It all started at that fundraiser, the night that I met you."

"Oh."

"That's where I met Aaron."

Tiffany tried to think back but drew a blank. "Aaron who?"

"You don't know him? Aaron Cordon. He's the director of the Washington Parks Department."

Tiffany frowned and pulled out her phone. "The name sounds familiar – hang on a second."

She searched for him online and pulled up his profile on the parks website. "It says here that he's an *assistant* director."

"Oh," said Rachel. "Great. Another way he tricked me."

"How did he trick you?" asked Tiffany. She navigated to Aaron's Facebook page as she listened.

Now she remembered looking at his profile – he was one of the least professional people she'd stalked. A lot of his pictures were of him partying or surrounded by beautiful women. Tiffany remembered thinking it was odd but nothing too unusual for a guy his age.

Ha – his age. She was starting to sound like a grandma; the guy was probably only a few years younger than she was.

"Well I was honestly just trying to follow Sidney's advice when I went to talk to him at the Milky Way Star Awards. I knew that Aaron worked for the parks department...and yeah, I guess I thought he was cute, too."

Tiffany didn't agree, but she could see the appeal. "Okay."

"He told me that he was the director and in charge of all this important stuff, but that he was just using it as a stepping stone for the rest of his career. And he said all this stuff about how he could show me what great things I could achieve."

"Ah, so he talked himself up." Tiffany was familiar with this particular type of blowhard – the young, barely successful blowhard. She'd met a lot in her day.

"Yeah." Rachel wiped her nose on the back of her hand. "I know. I'm so stupid."

"You're not stupid. Don't say that about yourself, okay?"

Rachel nodded.

"So what happened?"

"Well, he got my number and he would send me pictures of himself at all of these really fancy events. He just seemed like, I don't know, so cool. He offered to bring me to this fundraiser today and said that it would be really good experience for my future, and that he really liked me..."

"I think I see where this is going."

She looked down at her hands. "I don't know, I thought it sounded really cool and that maybe I would learn something? And we flew here in a *private* plane!"

Rachel paused for effect.

"Oh. *Oh!*" Tiffany nodded. She was far too old to fall for something like that, but she knew that her eighteen-year-old self would have been quite dazzled.

"So I thought he was like, really legit. And we get to this fundraiser and we're having fun for like two hours when this lady comes over – this senator lady, and she was so mad and pulled him aside."

"Wait – do you know who that was?"

Rachel sighed. "He called her Senator Shields? I think? I remembered it because I had a gym teacher with the same last name in high school. Anyway, after he came back he said that I needed to leave and he just pushed me outside of the hotel!"

"Wow. That's awful."

"I just felt so dumb for coming out here and I have no way to get home and if Sidney finds out..."

Tiffany reached out and put a hand on Rachel's shoulder. "Listen – I know that Sidney really cares about you. And if he's hard on you, it's just because he doesn't know how else to keep you safe."

Rachel sighed and appeared to be clenching her jaw.

Tiffany kept talking. "But he also doesn't know what it's like to be young and trying to find your place in the world."

"No, because he's always done everything right."

Tiffany laughed. "I'm not sure that that's true. And I do think that you should tell him about this – when you're ready. You need to be honest with him."

"You promised you wouldn't tell!"

Tiffany nodded. "And I won't. But I'm just saying – once you get over the shock of this, you need to talk to him."

She crossed her arms. "I'll think about it."

"I'll give you a ride home – but you owe me one," Tiffany said, pointing a finger at her.

"All right, that's fair," Rachel replied.

Tiffany was just about to ask for Rachel's address to put into the GPS when her phone rang. Her stomach dropped when she saw who it was – Sidney!

Chapter 18

The phone rang several times; Sidney thought that it might go to voicemail, but Tiffany picked up at the last second.

"Hello?"

"Hey, Tiffany. It's Sidney, how are you?"

"Hey Sidney." She let out a sigh. "I'm so sorry to do this, but I have to cancel our plans for tonight."

"Oh? Is everything okay?"

"Uh, yeah. Something unexpected came up and – I'm really sorry."

"Maybe we can reschedule next week?"

"Yeah! Definitely. I have to run, but I'll talk to you soon?"

"Sure. Take care."

He sat for a moment, muddling through his confusion. She sounded...off. Almost suspicious. What was going on? Was it something to do with the trial?

If it was, why couldn't she just tell him that? She didn't offer any excuse, actually. That was odd.

He sat in his office feeling stunned for about a half hour before he realized that he needed to call the restaurant and cancel their reservation.

The more he thought about her canceling, the less sense it made. He went to the website for the San Juan Island newspaper to see what happened at the trial. The article described two new bombshells – apparently, the defendant accused her boyfriend of the crime, and then he came back and accused *her,* showing up with new evidence.

Huh. That all seemed quite exciting; so Tiffany's cancellation must have been something to do with it.

But what? Maybe she wasn't allowed to talk about it?

No, that didn't make any sense; only the jury wasn't allowed to talk about an ongoing trial.

Whatever. It didn't matter – now he could stay late and catch up on a few things. It was fine. They'd reschedule, and hopefully she could tell him what had happened.

By eight o'clock, his eyes were tired of staring at his computer screen and he was about to head home when an email popped up from Eric. He frowned when he saw the subject line – FWD: How about some friendly competition, Burke?

It was an email from Eric's old classmate Steve. Eric never really liked the guy, but he had to be polite with him because their paths often crossed, both personally and professionally.

Sidney had a hard time tolerating Steve and usually avoided speaking to him whenever possible. In Sidney's view, Steve had all of the same advantages that Eric had – private schooling, wealth, an Ivy League education. But he had none of the good humor, charm or kindness that Eric possessed, and it made him completely unbearable.

"Hey Sidney," wrote Eric at the top of the email. "Bad news. It looks like Steve is coming after our project."

He scrolled down to see that Steve attached a picture of a model for a build on San Juan Island. He boasted that he had suppliers that would cut his costs by thirty percent, and that Burke Development had no chance to compete with him.

"I got my bid in a little late," wrote Steve. "But I'm pretty happy with the results."

Thirty percent less? "Yeah, if everything's falling off the back of a truck..." Sidney muttered to himself.

There was no way that Steve was doing any of this above board. With insurance and labor costs, he had to be cutting corners somewhere. It didn't make any sense.

Except now, everything made sense. Tiffany and Jade must've just gotten this bid and were seriously considering it. That's why Tiffany was acting strangely.

Sidney tried to keep himself from getting angry. Maybe that wasn't the reason that she canceled. Yet somehow he couldn't come up with anything else that would cause Tiffany to act this way – and all so suddenly. As far as he knew, the only thing that changed was this bid from Steve.

Of course it couldn't have been their decision entirely; there was an entire committee and representatives from the county to think about. So it wasn't necessarily true that Jade or Tiffany were to blame if they went with Steve's company instead.

But still, why couldn't Tiffany have just told him that? Why did she have to cancel their dinner plans and act so fishy?

Was she planning to use this bid to drive their offer down? In normal circumstances that might've worked, but Steve was offering fantasy prices, and they couldn't compete with that.

Sidney shut off his computer and started walking to his car. He kept telling himself not to get upset and that it was just business, but he couldn't get himself to actually believe it.

It wasn't just business with Tiffany. That was his mistake – he'd trusted her. He thought that she was honest. He thought that she was genuine.

But here it was. Even going to dinner with him was probably a shrewd business decision on her part.

He was right about her the first time he met her – he should've trusted his gut with his first impression.

But no, instead he let his guard down. How could he have fallen for that? When had *anything* good ever come out of letting his guard down?

By the time Sidney got home, he'd formulated a plan and responded to Eric's email.

"We don't need this. Tomorrow I'm going to send you a list of ten new potential projects, and you're going to pick your top five. We are moving on."

Then he shut off his phone and went for a run, determined to forget that the past week had even happened.

Chapter 19

That night, Tiffany didn't get back from dropping Rachel off in Seattle until midnight. She ended up missing the last ferry back to Friday Harbor, but Chief Hank generously offered to pick her up in his boat and bring her home.

She had to leave Jade's car on the mainland, and while Jade assured her that she didn't mind, Tiffany felt terrible about all of it. Her only relief was getting to bed that night; she fell asleep instantly.

The events of the night left her feeling uneasy, though, and she woke up early. Everything was running through her mind – abandoning Jade's car, Chief having to pick her up, and of course, canceling on Sidney and not telling him about Rachel. She was able to catch the early ferry to Anacortes and bring Jade's car back, so that made her feel a bit better.

Also, Rachel sent her a message that morning thanking her for her help again. That was nice...but Tiffany felt like she still had a long way to set things right again.

On her way back into town, she picked up some donuts and pastries from the bakery to bring to her mom's house. Since Ronny was staying there, it became a sort of trial head-quarters. Morgan and Jade were already there when Tiffany arrived.

"You've had a busy morning," said Jade.

Tiffany rubbed her face. "It's been a busy twenty four hours."

"Are those for me?" asked Morgan, staring at the box from the bakery.

"Yeah! But Chief gets first pick, because he came to rescue me last night when I got stranded."

"Finally!" Chief came over and peered into the box. "The recognition that I deserve."

Tiffany laughed. "I really appreciated your help. Thank you again."

"Any time. Really." His hand hovered over the box before choosing a jelly-filled donut. "I don't want to hear any jokes about the cop picking a donut."

They all laughed and Tiffany set the box down on the dining room table.

Morgan picked up a croissant and sat down next to her dad. "Unfortunately, I have to meet with a client today."

"Can you cancel?" asked Jade.

"No, I really shouldn't. It's not a big deal, and maybe it'll be good to think about something else for a bit."

Chief turned to Ronny. "In that case, can I interest you in some fishing today?"

"Oh sure," Ronny said. "That sounds great, actually."

"Would anyone else like to join?" asked Chief.

Tiffany, her mom, and Jade all looked at each other.

"We'll pass," said Jade.

Her mom got busy with packing a picnic for the fishermen, and Tiffany and Jade sat down on the couch with their coffees.

"I feel really bad about canceling on Sidney," Tiffany said. "And about helping to cover up Rachel's excursion."

Jade nodded. "Yeah, Rachel put you in a tough position. Can you just tell him it was a family emergency?"

"I could, but that's not really the truth. Although...it was an emergency with *his* family?" Tiffany shook her head. "No, that doesn't work. I tried calling him this morning, but he didn't pick up."

Jade bit her lip. "Do you think he's mad?"

"Maybe. I mean – probably. I canceled at the last minute."

"Can you send him a text and tell him when you're free next week?"

"Yeah...maybe we can go out on Friday? I just hope that the jury is done by then."

Jade groaned. "They need to be done by then. Waiting around is so stressful."

"I know." Tiffany set her coffee down. "Oh! I completely forgot to tell you – you know how Rachel was at the fundraiser with that guy Aaron?"

"Yeah?"

"Well apparently, he only kicked her out after he talked to a Senator...Shields, I think?"

Jade frowned. "Who's that? Do you think she was mad because Rachel wasn't allowed to be there, or something?"

"I don't know, I don't think so. Rachel said that she seemed to get angry when she looked at her – and gave her a really dirty look."

"Weird. I wonder what her problem was?"

Tiffany did a search on her phone and found the senator online. "Here she is – Senator Kathy Shields."

"Hm. I don't know much about her."

"I'm not sure what to make of it," Tiffany said with a shrug. "The whole situation is weird. I mean, Aaron is your run-of-the-mill arrogant jerk. But what could this senator possibly have said to make him stick Rachel outside with no way to get home?"

"That was ridiculous," Jade said. "I wish I could file a complaint with the parks department."

"I don't think he'd get in trouble for being a bad date, no matter how terrible it was. And Rachel doesn't want anything getting back to Sidney."

Jade was on her phone, swiping through pictures of the senator when she gasped.

"What?" asked Tiffany.

"Look!" Jade held up her phone. "She has a picture with Jared!"

Tiffany's eyes widened. It looked like a smarmy event. Jared's pinched, smug face stared back at her, smiling with that signature dead-eyed smile. If there was anyone in the world that Tiffany hated, it was the guy who was responsible for almost burning her sister's house down and killing her. "It looks like this lady keeps some *very* poor company."

Jade nodded and set her phone down. "Yeah, this makes me feel a little sick, actually, to see them together."

"I don't know who this lady is, but now I *know* she's up to no good."

"Do you think this senator might have something to do with that super PAC that Sidney found?"

"Good question. I don't remember seeing her name, but I'll double check." Tiffany pulled up the donation list for the super PAC. "Oh look – there's more stuff in here now."

"Oh!" Jade leaned over to get a better look. "I knew that they had to update who they're donating to every so often. Quarterly, or yearly? I'm not sure."

Tiffany gasped. "Oh my gosh Jade, look! There she is – Kathy Shields!"

"Look how much money they put into her campaign."

"Twelve *million* dollars? Are you kidding me!"

Jade set her coffee down. "This is crazy – way too crazy to be a coincidence."

"I know. I have to call Sidney. I just won't mention anything about her knowing Aaron..."

Jade nodded. "Good luck with that."

Tiffany dialed Sidney's number again – no answer. She frowned. "I think he's ignoring me."

"He might just be busy. Does he usually answer pretty quickly?"

Tiffany sighed. "He usually answers right away."

Jade made a face. "Well...that's not great."

Tiffany groaned. "Ugh. Now what are we going to do? I don't know the name of that forensic accountant that he was working with."

"Well..." Jade said slowly. "You could ask Dad."

Tiffany scoffed. "No thanks."

"He's had a really rough year. Did you know that his company went bankrupt?"

"So?"

"I'm not defending him – I'm really not. But I think that losing the company he spent his entire life building has really woken him up. He regrets that he put so much time and effort into it. He told me that."

"Jade, I'm sorry, but I'm not going to feel sympathy for him. I'm just not."

Jade nodded. "All right. Maybe Sidney will get back to you soon."

"Yeah, once he gets back to me, we can figure this out."

Saturday rolled into Sunday, and it became increasingly clear that Sidney was definitely ignoring her. Was he really *that* sensitive about her canceling their plans? Or...had he found out about her hiding Rachel's whereabouts from him?

Tiffany sent a text message to Rachel asking if Sidney knew what they'd been up to on Friday.

"No, I don't think so. Why?"

"He's not speaking to me," Tiffany wrote back. "And I'd like to know what he's mad about."

"Good luck with that!" wrote Rachel. "He can be mad for days. Weeks, even!"

Well, that wasn't helpful. She decided to go straight to the source and typed out a message to Sidney. "Hey, I'm really sorry about canceling on Friday. I wish I could tell you what was going on, but it's not my secret to share. I can only hope that if (and when) you find out, you won't be angry at me. Can we please talk?"

He wrote back a few minutes later. "I understand. Things are very busy for me right now, so don't worry about it."

She let out a groan. How had she managed to mess *everything* up?

Chapter 20

On Sunday evening, Sidney stopped by Eric's house; he needed to get an answer from him about new projects, and dropping in on him seemed to be the best way to do it.

"I wish you'd come a little earlier," Eric's wife Agatha said as she opened the door. "You could've had dinner with us – and the kids love seeing you."

Sidney smiled. "Maybe next time, I'm sorry Aggie."

"Yes, next time you're not getting out of it!" She stepped aside to let him into the house. "I've got to give the kids a bath and put them to bed, but I'll go find Eric and tell him that you're here."

"Thank you."

Eric came down the stairs a moment later. "Hey cousin! Nice to see you."

"Nice to see you too. I assume you know why I'm here."

"To bring me flowers?"

Sidney laughed. "No."

"All right, I know," Eric said, waving Sidney to follow him to the kitchen. "I looked at those other projects that you sent me – but nothing's jumping out."

Sidney sighed. "I'm sorry Eric, but you have to pick one. You can't keep hoping that things will work out with the San Juan project."

Eric crossed his arms. "Wait a minute, how was dinner on Friday? Did you ask Tiffany about Steve's bid?"

"No. She canceled."

Eric frowned. "Oh. I hope nothing's wrong."

"I think it's pretty obvious that they've decided to go with Steve – if they go with anyone at all. So we need to move on."

"I don't think Jade would do that without telling me. I think we just need to talk to her. But then again, I didn't want to bother her while she's dealing with her sister's trial. Have you seen? It's been all over the news."

Sidney nodded. "I have, but I don't think that's the issue. Eric, your dad was very clear that – "

He put up a hand. "Let me worry about my dad. Can't you just ask Tiffany what's going on?"

"No."

"Why not?"

"Because I *can't!*" Sidney stopped himself before he said any more – he shouldn't raise his voice like that, especially with kids in the house. "I'm sorry. I didn't mean to – "

"It's all right." Eric put his hands up. "Hey, can I get you something to drink? Are you hungry?"

"No, I'm fine." He sighed. "I'm worried about what we're going to do, and I feel like I'm losing my mind because I'm the only one thinking about it."

"I think about it all the time! I just trust that something's going to work out."

"Things don't just work out on their own, Eric. We need to figure them out, we need to plan, we need to – "

"I'm not ready to give up on our San Juan project yet."

"Whether you're ready or not, it's over. I'm sorry, but it's obvious."

Eric leaned against the kitchen island. "Do you really think so? I can't believe that Jade would change her mind like that and not tell me."

"But Tiffany would. She's a lot sharper than she looks. She had me fooled."

Eric reached into the fridge and pulled out a can of grape soda. "I've got your favorite," he said, in a sing-song voice.

Sidney smiled and accepted it. "Thanks."

"Let's sit."

Sidney obliged, sitting across from him on the couch.

Eric took a deep breath before starting again. "I need to say something to you without you getting upset with me."

He cracked the soda open. "Fine."

"Do you think that you *might* be overreacting a little bit about Tiffany?"

Sidney crossed his arms. "No. She betrayed my trust. There's no coming back from that."

"I mean, maybe. You don't even know for sure what's going on. You know – you can't assume every woman who catches your eye is as cold and calculating as Priscilla."

Sidney took a swig of the grape soda. He wondered if the kids were allowed to drink this stuff, or if Eric kept it for himself. It was horrible – so full of sugar. But it tasted like home. "That's not what's happening here."

Eric put his hands up. "Okay! Just putting it out there."

"Can you please just promise to pick a project by the end of the week?"

Eric shrugged. "All right, I will."

"Thanks." Sidney stood, finishing off the rest of the soda before tossing the can into the recycling bin. "I've got work to do tonight, but I'll see you tomorrow?"

Eric nodded. "Sure."

Sidney got home and had a hard time focusing on work. Eric was wrong; Priscilla didn't have a hold on him anymore –

he'd proven that the last time he saw her. He was his own man now, and he wouldn't let a heartbreak from ten years ago mess with him.

Of course the experience had changed him; but a lot had changed him over the years. And he'd learned that there were very few people that he could actually count on.

It was foolish of him to think that Tiffany could be one of those people after only knowing her for so short a time. Her apparent honesty disarmed him, her wit charmed him, and she was stunningly beautiful – but none of that meant he should have let his guard down with her.

He could at least thank Tiffany for the lesson. He would never make that mistake again.

Chapter 21

When her alarm went off on Monday, Morgan was already awake. She'd woken up about an hour prior, surprised that she'd managed to sleep at all.

For most of the weekend, she was able to focus on things other than her mom's trial. Work kept her distracted on Saturday, and on Sunday, Luke insisted that she go rock climbing with him. Afterwards, Margie made everyone a big dinner and it was easy to get lost in the conversation and laughter.

But now her nerves were back in full force. She got out of bed and quietly got ready before slipping outside.

It was a gorgeous, clear day and Morgan closed her eyes, trying to enjoy the calm of the morning. The birds were happily chirping away – perhaps she'd just stand here all day and watch them?

But no – after a few minutes, Luke pulled up in his old, beat up car.

"Are you sure we shouldn't take my car?" she asked as she got in, kissing him on the cheek.

"No! I *specifically* cleaned it to impress your dad! Do you smell that?"

She frowned. "Yeah, what is that?"

He pointed to the hanging air freshener. "Orange popsicle."

"Oh in that case, never mind," she said with a laugh. "He needs to experience this."

Luke had been such a steadfast support through all of this, doing whatever was needed, often without being asked. He chauffeured, he cooked, and best of all, he made her laugh.

She reached over and took hold of his hand. He smiled at her and squeezed back before reversing down the driveway and heading toward Margie's house.

On the ride over, Morgan was quiet and absorbed in her thoughts. They still had no idea how long it would take for the jury to deliberate – it could be hours or days before they came to a decision.

Morgan had insisted that everyone else stay home and not spend their days waiting in the courtroom. They had jobs and lives to get back to, and she already felt like they'd done too much.

When they arrived at Margie's house, her dad was ready to go and was in good spirits.

"Remember honey – we only need to take this one day at a time."

"I know Dad, I'm just...so tired of not knowing what's going to happen."

"Yeah. But your mom wouldn't have wanted you to be so upset. Look what I picked up when I was in town with Hank."

Morgan watched him pull a deck of Uno cards from his pocket.

"*Dad*, we are not going to sit in the courtroom and play Uno!"

"Oh, here you're wrong," said Luke. "Because if my vote counts, we are *definitely* going to be playing Uno, and I am going to win."

She shook her head, smiling, and decided not to argue.

It didn't take long to get to the courthouse, and though Morgan initially planned to get breakfast nearby, Margie thwarted those plans by sending along freshly made breakfast sandwiches on homemade biscuits.

They were on their third game of Uno when Morgan got a call from Leo.

"Hey Morgan. I just got word and I'm coming to the courthouse. The jury has reached a verdict."

"Oh my gosh! Thank you – I'm already here. See you soon."

"Great!"

Morgan sent out text messages to Margie, Jade, and Tiffany before going into the courtroom and getting back to her regular seat.

The next half hour felt like it was in slow motion. The courtroom began to fill with people – not just the ones she was hoping to see, but also reporters and strangers.

Notably, Brock was nowhere to be seen. Luke thought he had probably spent the entire weekend doing damage control after turning on Andrea. He said it would be a big hit on Brock's business interests, which is probably why he resisted turning on her sooner.

Both Matthew and Chief, though they were currently on the clock, were able to make it to the courthouse and took their seats. By the time the judge asked everyone to rise for the jury's entrance, Morgan had her entire crew by her side.

"Good morning everyone. I'd like to remind you all that I expect quiet and order in my courtroom. Now, who was our foreperson, juror number two?"

A male juror responded – one Morgan had nicknamed Mr. Blue Glasses. She'd always liked him. "Yes Your Honor."

"Has the jury reached a verdict?"

"We have, Your Honor," said Mr. Blue Glasses.

"Please stand and read the verdict to the court."

The man rose from his seat, eyes focused on the paper he had in front of him.

He didn't make eye contact with anyone. Was that a bad sign?

Morgan gripped one cold, clammy hand onto Luke and the other cold, clammy hand onto her dad. Her heart was thundering away in her chest and she really regretted eating those breakfast sandwiches – her stomach felt more uneasy with every passing moment.

"The State of Washington versus Andrea Collins, case 803. Verdict – count one, vehicular homicide. We, the Jury, find the defendant, Andrea Collins, guilty."

A cry escaped from the back of the courtroom; Morgan didn't turn around to see who it was, though. A chill ran over her body and she turned toward her dad, tears in her eyes, and hugged him.

The emotional outburst behind them continued until Judge Gore struck his gavel. "Please compose yourself or you'll be removed from the courtroom."

The noise died down and he spoke again.

"The jury having rendered this verdict, and considering that Andrea Collins now stands convicted, I am revoking her bond and remand her to the county jail until sentencing, which I will set to ninety days from today. Adjourned until ninety days from now."

Morgan watched as Andrea broke her hug with Rudy, turning around with tears streaming down her face. She stood like that for a moment, but no one came to comfort her. She was placed in handcuffs and led away.

While everyone chatted excitedly, Morgan looked to the other side of the courtroom. It didn't appear that any of Andrea's family returned for the reading of the verdict.

She could see that a woman was holding up a cell phone on a video call; it looked like she was talking to Andrea's father. The only thing that Morgan caught from the conversation was him saying that Andrea was "a disappointment."

Even though Morgan agreed with him, she couldn't help but feel sad for Andrea. Andrea had taken Morgan's mother away and ripped their family apart – but it seemed like Andrea didn't have a family to begin with.

Morgan had to shelve these unexpected feelings because the next hour was a blur. They talked to Leo and thanked him for all of his hard work on the case. He then told them what the next steps would be as far as sentencing and what they might expect.

When they walked out of the courthouse, there were two reporters trying to speak to them. Morgan was too stunned to react, but luckily Luke navigated her back to the car and took her back to Margie's.

Once there, they were enjoying some of Margie's ever available wonderful cooking when Morgan finally had a chance to talk to her dad alone.

"Is it weird that I feel...kind of bad for Andrea?"

Her dad shook his head. "No, it's not weird. It means that you're human."

"I mean, I still wanted her to be found guilty. Because if she had just gotten away with it, the way that she gets away with everything in her life...I don't know. That would be so unjust."

"I feel the same way. And I hope the judge gives her a fair sentence," her dad said. "I'd like to think that she'll learn something. But I'm not going to hold my breath."

Morgan nodded. "Yeah. Maybe someday she'll feel as sorry for Mom as she does for herself."

"Unfortunately, compassion is a difficult lesson to teach."

Morgan let out a sigh. "I guess you're right. Well – I'm glad it's over."

"Me too."

Morgan joined Jade and Tiffany at the table and thanked them again for taking so much time out of their lives to be there for her.

"Of course, we will *always* be here when you need us," Jade said.

"And we'll be here even when you really don't want us around," Tiffany added with a smile.

Morgan laughed. "I'm sorry I've been so absent from everything else going on. Tiffany – how was your date with Sidney?"

She groaned. "Not good. It didn't happen. I had to drive Rachel all the way back to Seattle and I couldn't tell him what I was doing."

"Oh no!"

"He's been ignoring me, so I'm thinking that I might stop by his office tomorrow and force him to talk."

Morgan slowly nodded. "I approve of this plan. Were you able to find anything else out about that senator?"

Jade cleared her throat. "Kind of...and my dad had some ideas."

Tiffany turned toward her. "Jade! How do you think Morgan would feel if we started working with the man who abandoned her?"

"I don't know, why don't you ask her?"

Morgan smiled. "Yeah Tiffany, why don't you ask me?"

Tiffany sighed. "Because I don't want to hurt your feelings. I'm never going to side with my dad over you. What he did to you was – "

"It was bad, yeah," Morgan said, putting up a hand. "But to tell you the truth...it's not like I'm still holding it against him. I didn't even know that he existed for most of my life. And I have a dad. A great one."

Tiffany bit her lip. "I don't know why, but that makes me want to cry."

"Don't cry!" Morgan hugged her. "I'm sorry that your dad's a jerk. I honestly wish you could find some peace with it. Don't hold a grudge on my account."

Tiffany leaned back, her eyes wide. "Who *are* you?"

"I'm serious," Morgan said with a laugh. "I even felt bad for Andrea today. I don't know, I think I'm growing up or something."

Tiffany put a hand to her forehead. "Are you sure you don't have a fever?"

"I think she's perfectly fine," said Jade. "And I already knew that she felt this way, but I thought you should hear it straight from her."

Morgan nodded. "Please – if your dad could help figure out the funding for this project, by all means, talk to him! And if he wants to make up with you – "

"But what if he wants to make up with *you*?" asked Tiffany.

Morgan shrugged. "I don't know. I honestly don't really care about him. What is it that they say about anger? That it's like hanging onto a hot coal that you're planning to throw at somebody else?"

Tiffany laughed. "Something like that."

"Well yeah, that's how I feel about him. I already publicly ruined his birthday party, revenge doesn't really get any better than that."

They all laughed and Margie arrived holding a plate of cookies, asking what was so funny. Tiffany tried to explain, poorly, and ended up being handed three cookies.

Morgan sat back and looked at the scene in front of her. There were times when she thought that she'd never get answers for her mom's death, but here she was. Surrounded by the ones she loved the most, and with an odd feeling of peace in her heart.

It was over, it was done. It was finally okay for her to move on.

Chapter 22

Somehow, Tiffany managed to schedule a meeting with Sidney on Tuesday. When she initially contacted his assistant, an automated message shot back saying that she was out of the office and that another employee was covering her emails.

That was Tiffany's way in – this other person didn't even know who she was, so she assured them that Sidney wanted to meet and that it needed to be as soon as possible.

On the drive down to Seattle, she went over different scenarios in her head. The worst of all would be if he saw her on his schedule and refused to meet with her; the second worst would be if he talked to her and pretended like nothing had happened. That seemed more likely.

She arrived at the Burke Industries building, an impressive high-rise, and was able to park in the garage. Once upstairs, she sat in a swanky looking waiting room and was offered espresso and champagne.

"I'm fine, thank you," she said. Clearly Eric's hospitality and showmanship came from his father. These people tried to give *everyone* champagne.

She was scheduled to meet with Sidney at eleven, and when she wasn't immediately called back, she started getting nervous. Maybe he would just completely ignore her?

But after five minutes, she got her chance – Sidney was just walking through the lobby when she spotted him. He stopped dead in his tracks.

"Tiffany?" he said, brow furrowed.

She stood up. "Hey!"

"I'm running late for my next meeting – "

She nodded. "I know, it's with me."

"Ah." He stared at her for a beat. "Well, come on in."

She followed him into his office and tried not to gawk too much at the decorations and the beautiful view.

He sat down at his desk, fussing with a pile of papers for a moment. Tiffany watched him – he clearly had his armor back on. It wasn't just the suit and tie; it was also his flat and serious expression. Morgan would probably call him a stink face, actually. He looked very different from the man who took her boating last week.

"How can I help you?" he asked finally, sitting back in his chair.

Tiffany scooted to the edge of her seat. "Well first, I want to apologize again for canceling last week."

"It's fine, no harm done."

He said it so easily that she *almost* believed him.

"It's clearly not fine, because you've been ignoring me. Come on Sidney – I'll admit that I let you down."

He crossed his arms. "Okay. Can you tell me the reason now? Why you were suddenly unavailable?"

She folded her hands in her lap. "No, I can't."

He nodded. "Am I right in thinking that it had something to do with the stalled project on San Juan Island?"

Hm. She still hoped that Rachel would come clean to Sidney eventually, so she didn't want to lie to him. "It's not *completely* unrelated. Actually, I found something else out about the funding and – "

"I think this is a good time to let you know that we've decided to go in another direction. Eric and I."

"Oh?" Tiffany sat back. "I mean, I understand if you can't wait for the funding to come through, but – "

"I believe that it's important to have partners that are reliable. In business."

"Right." Tiffany paused for a moment, staring into his eyes before repeating, "In business."

He stood up, breaking the eye contact and buttoning his suit jacket. "But I wish you the best of luck with the project. I have to get going."

"Sidney – please."

He turned around. "Say hello to Steve for me."

She stared at him blankly. "Steve?"

But he was already showing her out, and she could see another person already eagerly waiting at the door.

Tiffany collected herself, thanked him for taking the time to meet with her and walked past him.

"You're welcome," he said politely before shutting the door behind her.

When Tiffany got back to her car, she called Jade.

"Hey! How'd it go?"

"Not well," said Tiffany. "He thinks I'm unreliable and said that they're moving on to other projects."

"No! Maybe I can call Eric and talk to him?"

"You can, but what are we going to pay them with?" said Tiffany. "And do you know anyone named Steve?"

"No, why? Oh..." Jade groaned. "Wait."

"What?"

"Yeah, I think I *do* know a Steve – why, did Sidney say something?"

"He told me to say hi to Steve and I have no idea what he was talking about."

"All right, this is my fault. I got this really weird call last week from this guy named Steve. He sent in a bid for the park."

"Go on..."

"It was strange – like it wasn't good at all. There were all these 'special rates' and it seemed shady. Plus he was annoying on the phone, and he kinda creeped me out. I didn't think anything of it, and we were so busy with the trial that I forgot to tell you guys."

Tiffany sighed. "Okay, this is making more sense now."

"Does he really think that we'd go with someone like that? And behind his back?"

"Apparently." Tiffany sat for a moment, thinking. "But it doesn't matter, because we can't go with *anyone* right now."

"I don't know what to do," said Jade. "I really don't."

"Ugh. All right. I'm going to make the call."

"What call?"

"To Dad."

There was silence for a moment. "Wow. All right – good luck."

"Thanks."

Tiffany drove along for another forty minutes before finally giving in and calling her dad. She was trying to think of anything else they could possibly do, but kept coming up empty-handed.

He picked up right away.

"Tiffany! How are you?"

"Hi."

"It's so good to hear from you."

Yeah, whatever. "I was wondering if you could help me with something."

"Anything."

"Has Jade told you about our troubles with the park?"

"Yeah – I talked to her a few weeks ago. Are you still running into issues?"

"Yeah." She let out a sigh and explained the details of the funding, the super PAC, and the odd fundraising for Senator Shields.

"That's all interesting," he said. "If I had to guess, it sounds like pretty standard embezzlement, maybe by that parks employee."

"Aaron? But why?"

"Could be for political gain, a romantic affair, or he might just be plain power-hungry."

"Yeah, or maybe all of the above. So how do we prove it?"

"Well...that's where it gets tricky."

"How tricky?"

He sighed. "You can hand over any information you have to the authorities and hope that they have enough evidence to secure warrants and conduct an investigation."

"That sounds like it'll take forever."

"That's because it will. And he'll be counting on that. Plus, depending on what influence this senator has, she could make any scrutiny disappear in an instant."

"Oh come on, no way."

"Well...let's just say I've seen it happen."

Great. Her dad, the criminal, was really opening her eyes to the world. "So what then? We can't do anything and they just get away with this?"

"Well, no..."

Tiffany cleared her throat. "I assume that you have a lot of experience with embezzlement, Dad."

He was quiet for a moment. "I won't say that I'm proud of everything I've done in my career."

Tiffany rolled her eyes. "That's nice. How do we catch them?"

"Hang on. I need you to know some stuff. Did Jade tell you that I've lost the company? Chapter 11 bankruptcy."

"I've heard some things."

"I spent so many years building this business, thinking I'd have something to leave to you kids, and it's all gone. Just like that. And I have so many regrets – "

"Yeah, I heard."

He paused. "I understand that you're angry – I would be too. I don't expect you to forgive me for any of it. But I'm almost sixty years old and just now realizing what's important in life. It was never the business – it was you guys. You kids, and Mom."

"Well I think that ship has sailed, Dad."

"Just know that I'm here for you, okay? Anything that you need."

"What I need is proof of whatever fraud is going on so Jade's dreams don't get flushed down the toilet."

"Okay. I think I can help you with that. If you're willing to get...creative."

"I'm all ears."

Chapter 23

After Morgan dropped her dad off at the ferry terminal, she went back home and was surprised to see Jade and Tiffany sitting in the kitchen.

"Uh – why do you guys look like so serious?" she asked.

"Because Tiffany finally called our dad," Jade replied.

Morgan took a seat at the kitchen table. "And she made up with him and everything's okay now?"

"Ha, no." Tiffany said. "But he had an idea of how we could figure out if there's fraud in the parks department."

"Okay..." Morgan said slowly.

"But, it's what you *might* call a scheme. And it's not exactly above board."

Morgan smiled. "Oh I *love* a good scheme! I don't care what it is – I'm in."

"I don't know guys," Jade said. "And Morgan, you don't even know what it is yet!"

"Well," she shrugged. "I've already committed and I can't go back on my word now."

Tiffany laughed. "It really is kind of crazy. But my Dad seems to think it could work."

"Go on."

Tiffany set her coffee down. "All right. So my dad thinks that Aaron could be funneling money into that super PAC for the senator."

"But why?"

Tiffany shrugged. "Who knows. He thinks he's a hot shot, or it'll get him places. Or whatever. And the guy doesn't seem too bright. Or careful."

Jade interjected. "But that *doesn't* mean that this plan will work."

Morgan folded her arms across her chest. "Jade, you're one to talk. You pulled off a scheme and got Jared arrested and you didn't even tell us about it!"

"I know, but this is different. It seems...riskier."

Tiffany shook her head. "Not really. Okay, listen. Basically, the only reason my dad even suggested this plan is because it *actually* happened in his company. This guy showed up and – well, it's actually a big reason why they went bankrupt."

"That sounds serious," said Morgan.

"It was. So, a guy went to their office and pretended that he needed to update the printers."

"Like in your dad's actual office?" asked Morgan.

Tiffany nodded. "Yeah, but he wasn't working for my dad's company. He didn't work for anyone. But someone logged him into the computer system and even gave him the passwords he needed. Once he he was in, it was over. He extracted a bunch of information and now my dad might go to jail."

"That explains him trying to make amends," said Morgan.

Jade nodded. "I know, though I don't think he's going to end up going to jail. He's just going to end up losing all of his money."

"Which, for our dad," Tiffany added, leaning forward, "is *worse* than jail. Anyway – he said we could do the same thing. Get in there, pretend to have a legitimate need to get on the computer, and then try to find evidence of the fraud."

"That doesn't sound too hard," said Morgan.

"Are you kidding me?" Jade dropped her hands to the table. "We don't even know what we're looking for!"

"You're the computer person Jade," said Morgan. "Can't you just copy all the files and emails and stuff? And we'll figure it out later?"

Jade sighed. "I mean, kind of? It doesn't work like that. And you're assuming that he does all of his fraud on his work computer."

Morgan looked at Tiffany and then back at Jade. "I'd be willing to bet money that he does."

Tiffany smiled. "Me too, Morgan. We need Jade's computer skills, and we also need your charm."

She frowned. "Well, unfortunately I don't have much of that."

"We all have to be involved, but I'm afraid that Aaron could recognize one of us from the Milky Way Awards," said Jade. "I can do the computer stuff, but someone needs to distract him."

"Oh, you mean me?" Morgan clapped her hands together. "Oh my gosh – I kind of love this idea."

Tiffany turned toward Jade. "See? I told you that she'd be on board."

Jade held up a finger. "For the record, this is a bad idea."

Tiffany spun Jade's laptop around. "Look at this legit looking letter that Jade made."

Morgan leaned in. "3D Print-o-lab? Did you just make that up Jade?"

She nodded. "Yeah. Is it believable?"

"Yeah!"

"I was thinking we could present this to whatever staff is there and get on to Aaron's computer. If we're lucky, he may not even be there," Tiffany said.

Morgan nodded. "Sure. Tiffany, what's your role?"

"Waiting in the car, obviously, in case you need to run away.

"Yeah," Jade said with a frown. "I don't love the running away part."

"Don't worry," Tiffany said. "Dad just said we have to act like we belong there. And if anyone knows how to get away with things, it's him."

Jade put her hands on her face. "I can't believe we're doing this."

"Believe it sister!" Tiffany stood up. "I'm going to go and buy our uniforms."

Despite Jade's reservations, the next morning they packed into her car and caught the first ferry to the mainland. The state parks headquarters was in Olympia, a two and a half hour drive from Anacortes.

The drive there was a lot of fun, with Morgan practicing what she was going to say and also toying with her hairstyle.

"What do you think works better? Ponytail, or hair down?"

"I'm keeping my baseball hat on the entire time," said Jade. "I need to hide my face."

"I feel like the hat's not going to be flirty enough," Morgan mused. "I asked Luke his opinion yesterday."

Tiffany laughed. "Okay, first of all, no one said you had to flirt with the guy. And second of all...what did Luke say?"

"Oh he was *full* of advice, but none of it was very good. He said that I should wear a black dress, with high heels, and pretend that my car broke down and I needed help."

Jade laughed. "I mean, he gets points for trying, but that's an even worse plan than our current one."

"It's good that he wasn't jealous or anything," added Tiffany.

"Ha!" said Morgan. "I *wish* he would get jealous. Women hit on him *all the time*, and I have literally *never* had a guy hit on me when he's around. Or ever, come to think of it."

"You talk too much," Jade replied. "You scare them away."

Morgan's jaw dropped. "I would really resent that, if Luke hadn't essentially told me the same thing."

"In a nicer way, I hope?" asked Tiffany.

Morgan nodded. "Oh yeah, I think he said something like my mastery of the English language is intimidating to some men."

Jade laughed. "A very artful response from him. It's too bad that we couldn't have Luke go and hit on Aaron. He'd be perfect."

"I know, right?" Morgan sighed. "Don't worry – I'm going to channel my inner Luke. Maybe I should pretend that I'm new? Or an intern?"

"Hey," Jade protested. "I don't look *that* much older than you."

"Do whatever you need to do," said Tiffany. "Just give Jade enough time to find something."

They got to the building and Morgan tried to ignore the nervous butterflies in her stomach as she and Jade got out of the car.

Jade went to the trunk and pulled out a laptop bag and a large cardboard box.

"What's all that?" asked Morgan.

"Oh, just some supplies. My dad said to bring something to make ourselves look more professional."

Morgan picked up the box, surprised by how heavy it was. "What's in here?"

"Just an old printer with a plexiglas cube on top. You can't let anyone look at it for too long, or they might catch on to us."

Morgan nodded. "You got it boss."

Jade sighed and adjusted the strap of the laptop bag. "All right, let's go."

They walked into the unassuming office building. Morgan was surprised to see that there wasn't any security; then again, most people weren't trying to pull a fast one on the parks department.

They got on the elevator and rode up to the fifth floor where Aaron's office was listed. When the elevator doors opened, Morgan almost gasped. Aaron was just standing there, about to walk into the elevator. This was her time to shine!

She cleared her throat. "Excuse me?"

"Yes?" he said.

"We're supposed to install a 3D printer for a..." Morgan reached into her pocket and pulled out the fake order that Jade had designed. "An Aaron Corden? Do you have any idea how we could find his office?"

His face brightened and he stuck a hand against the elevator door to prevent it from closing. "That's me!"

"Oh, perfect!" said Morgan. "What great luck! I'm Janice, and this is...Barbie."

Jade smiled and waved. "Hi!"

"Nice to meet you. You can follow me. This is such great news. I had no idea I was getting a 3D printer. Did Chris order this?"

"I'm not sure," Morgan said. "We just do what we're told."

"Oh, right. Still, this is *sweet!*"

They followed him down the hall and into his office. Morgan felt giddy at how well it was going.

Sure, she'd blanked on their agreed-upon names and then could only think of calling Jade "Barbie," but other than that, it was going swimmingly!

"So parks, huh?" She wanted to keep Aaron looking at her so he wouldn't potentially recognize Jade, who was doing a very good job of keeping her face hidden under her hat. "I'm just interning right now with...Barbie. But maybe after school I could get a job here?"

"Uh – are you interested in parks?" he asked. "What are you going to school for?"

"Oh, uh, accounting."

No! *Why!* Why would she say that?

He smiled. "Oh, I work with them a good bit on the budget. I don't know if they're hiring, but there's always a spot for good people."

"I'll just need you to log into your computer so I can install the drivers," said Jade.

"Of course, no problem." He walked over and signed in, but then hovered behind Jade as she got to work.

Morgan racked her brain for a way to get him away from his office.

"Was that a map out there showing all of the state parks?"

He nodded. "Yep."

Darn. He didn't take the bait. "Cool. I'm sorry, but is there a bathroom around here? Would you mind showing me?"

"Oh – of course. The women's room is actually on the next floor down."

"Oh my gosh, I am *such* a klutz, I bet I'll get lost."

He hesitated for a moment. "Well, I can take you down?"

"If you don't mind!" She paused, deciding to risk a shoulder touch. "I'd really appreciate it."

He subtly pulled away from her hand and said, "Follow me."

Hm. First attempt at flirting did not go well. Maybe she'd tried to touch him too soon?

As they were waiting for the elevator, she tried chatting with him but got minimal response. He told her that he could wait for her outside of the bathroom.

She thanked him, but once she got inside, she felt panicked; should she actually go to the bathroom? Or just flush the toilet and wash her hands for a long time?

She decided to just flush the toilet and change her tactics. Flirting wasn't working.

"I really appreciate you helping me find my way down here. Every time I mess something up with Barbie, she makes it seem like I'm never going to be able to get a job."

"Really? She seems pretty nice."

"It's all an act," Morgan said. "She's actually really mean and I'm just desperate because I don't have any other options."

Aaron frowned. "That sucks, man. I know how it feels, my boss here isn't great either."

Bingo. "Oh really? What does he do?"

"He's just always after me and telling me that I'm not meeting expectations, but like, he doesn't make the expectations clear, you know?"

Morgan nodded, maybe a little bit too hard. "Oh yeah, totally."

"I mean, I don't want to kill your dreams of working at the parks department – "

"Oh, it's not, like, a real dream or anything. I just, you know, need to find a job."

"Yeah, I totally get it. That's why I'm here. I'm not going to be a lifer and waste my career here."

Morgan nodded again. "Yeah."

"Should we head back upstairs?"

She knew that she was supposed to get Jade as much time as she could, but she didn't know what else to say. "I mean, unless we can get a coffee or something? I can play hooky for a little bit longer."

Aaron smiled. "I like that attitude. Come on."

Perfect!

They went down to the lobby and both ordered drinks from a small coffee cart.

"Like this, for example," he said. "I almost closed a deal to franchise with a coffee shop for all the state parks and parks buildings."

"But your boss wouldn't allow it?"

"No! He said it was a conflict of interest – but I think that this coffee is a conflict of interest! It's terrible!"

Morgan forced herself not to make eye contact with the barista, who was probably glaring at them. "So he's really holding you back?"

Aaron took a sip of his coffee. "Yeah. It sucks. Whatever – I'm excited for this printer."

"Oh, yeah, they're really cool."

"Yeah."

They walked over to the elevator, and Morgan pulled out her phone and sent the warning signal to both Tiffany and Jade.

When they got back to the office, Jade already had her laptop packed up and the bag back on her shoulder.

"I'm really sorry, but your computer is actually too outdated for me to install what you'll need."

He groaned. "Are you serious?"

"Don't worry, this happens all the time," Morgan said. "We have an...older printer that we can bring."

"Right," said Jade. "We'll be in touch."

He crossed his arms. "All right, thanks for trying. It's typical that nothing works around here."

Morgan nodded. "Yeah, totally."

"Do you think that you can find your way out?"

"Yes, thanks!" Morgan called out over her shoulder, her voice going a little too high.

They skipped the elevator this time, instead running down the stairs and speed walking to the car where Tiffany was waiting.

Chapter 24

"Get in!" Tiffany hissed as she flung open the passenger side door.

Morgan hopped in while Jade slid into the backseat. As soon as they shut their car doors, Tiffany took off.

"How'd it go?' asked Tiffany.

"Okay," Jade said.

"Better than okay!" Morgan was almost shouting as she clicked into her seat belt. "I think our plan worked perfectly."

"Really?" They were at a red light and Tiffany turned to look at her. "Were you able to get onto his computer?"

"We were," Jade said from the back. "And he was the one who logged me onto it."

"No way!" Tiffany peeked at the GPS – it looked like they weren't going to hit much traffic. That was good – a clean escape. "And what, did Morgan get her chance to flirt with him?"

Jade laughed. "She tried, but he wasn't that receptive."

"Hang on," Morgan said. "That's not *entirely* fair! I mean – no, he wasn't interested in my advances. But he *did* want to gripe about his boss, and as a skilled flirt, I picked up on that and ran with it."

"Oh is *that* what you call it?" said Jade.

Morgan crossed her arms over her chest. "Yes, and you're welcome because when he and I got coffee together, I bought you a bunch of time. That was when he told me he was disgruntled that his boss wouldn't let him make money opening coffee shops in the state parks."

Tiffany frowned. "Wait, really? Is this guy really *that* dumb?"

"I'm afraid so," Morgan replied.

Tiffany shot a glance in the rearview mirror to Jade. "Did you find anything?"

"I'm just looking now. Let me dig through some things."

"What kind of crime is it for hacking a computer?" asked Morgan. "Is there jail time?"

Tiffany scoffed. "Well, if Jared only got three months of house arrest for conspiring to burn Jade's house down and almost killing her, then I doubt it."

"You'd be surprised," said Jade. "The legal system is not a fan of hackers. There have even been cases where hackers will pass information to journalists, and then the journalists are threatened with jail time to reveal who their source was."

"Wait," said Morgan. "You mean when the journalists are the ones doing the hacking?"

Jake shook her head. "No, the journalists get in trouble just for *receiving* the hacked documents. It's not good."

"So you're saying that if we get caught..." Tiffany paused. "We're toast?"

"Not exactly..." Jade replied. "I'm going to focus on looking at what we have here though."

"Okay." Tiffany really wished she knew how serious a crime this was *before* they went and did it.

Jade sat quietly in the back, sifting through the data she'd acquired. And Morgan took Tiffany's silence as an opportunity to tell her the play-by-play account of the visit to the state parks department headquarters.

Tiffany enjoyed Morgan's storytelling, but she was starting to get nervous. What if Jade didn't find anything, and they'd just committed computer fraud for no reason at all?

Or worse – what if they did find evidence of wrongdoing, but instead of Aaron being punished, *they* would be punished because they didn't have a senator on their side, and they'd gotten the evidence illegally?

"Did you see any cameras when you were in there?" asked Tiffany.

Morgan shrugged. "Not that I noticed. I looked around for them – there was nothing obvious."

"Okay, I guess that's good..." She sat there, driving and growing more nervous. "Maybe we should just throw that laptop into the ocean and never think about this again."

"Oh *now* you're scared?" said Jade. "I told you that this was a bad idea from the start."

Tiffany bit her lip. "I think you're right. I don't want to go to jail for this!"

Jade laughed. "We're not going to go to jail for this. I mean, probably. It's a misdemeanor."

"Is that a good thing?" asked Morgan.

"It's good that it's not a felony," said Jade. "We'd probably just end up with a fine."

"Do you think Leo would take my case?" Morgan said with a smile.

Tiffany ignored her. "But if we give something that we find to a journalist, will they get in trouble? Because it was stolen?"

Jade sighed. "I mean, journalists are supposed to be able to protect their sources. Usually that's how it works. But yeah, the concern is that if you go after someone powerful enough, they'll try to attack you in any way to protect themselves."

"I was *not* ready for this level of crime," Tiffany said. "I think that – "

"Don't get all worked up. The Supreme Court ruled that information, despite being stolen, can be published if it's a matter of public concern."

"Oh." Tiffany sat on that thought for a moment. "I'd say that this is a public concern. Especially if they're stealing from the taxpayers."

Jade gasped. "Oh my gosh! Here it is!"

"What?" Morgan and Tiffany asked at the same time.

"It's all right here, in his email! Seriously, just *everything*. Are all criminals *this* dumb?" asked Jade.

"I watch a lot of true crime documentaries," said Morgan, "and based on that, I'd say that a lot of them *are* really dumb. I'm sure there are ones who are smart enough not to get caught though and those are the ones you need to worry about..."

"What does it say?" asked Tiffany.

"There are a ton of emails between him and Senator Shields. Tiffany, you were right – they were having a *truly* torrid love affair. I mean, some of these emails are – "

Tiffany held up a hand. "Please, spare us the details."

"Sure, sorry. But I can't believe it – it's all spelled out here. She was angry and jealous that he showed up with Rachel at that fundraiser, and he promised her that he was just doing a favor for a friend in bringing along Rachel. He said she was his friend's little sister."

"There is no way that Sidney is friends with Aaron," Tiffany said firmly.

"No, of course not. But he *is* friends with Jared – they've emailed back and forth. And it looks like after the fundraiser, Aaron sent Senator Shields flowers..." Jade clicked around. "And assured her that he only had eyes for her..."

"Ew," Morgan said. "Isn't she like ten years older than him?"

"Try sixteen years older," said Jade. "Not that I have anything against a healthy relationship with an age gap!"

Tiffany laughed. "No one thinks you're an ageist, Jade. But clearly, he wasn't in a relationship with her because he liked her."

Jade nodded. "Yeah. That's pretty obvious. He talks about all of the money that he's going to make available for her campaign. He even mentioned the super PAC by name!"

"Wow, he really is an idiot," said Tiffany.

"I think people get arrogant and cocky. They think they're outsmarting everybody and they behave like this," said Morgan.

Tiffany shrugged. "I guess you're right. So what can we do with this now?"

"Leave that to me," said Jade. "I have a friend who's a journalist. I trust her – if I give her this information, I trust that she'll protect my identity."

Tiffany cringed. "Can't you just send it anonymously?"

"I could, but then she'll have to spend a lot of time and resources verifying that it's legitimate. If I tell her that I went and got these emails myself..."

Morgan giggled. "Your friend *might* die of shock."

"Yeah, that's true." Jade laughed. "But she'd know that I'm telling the truth. And then...she could run with the story."

By the time they got to the ferry, Jade's mind was made up about her plan. She said that she was disgusted by Aaron's behavior and how he was ruining the state parks department for generations to come.

"This is about more than just my park," she said. "This bonehead is stealing from the state and stealing from us all! How could he do this?"

Tiffany shrugged. "Scammers are gonna scam."

"And they would've gotten away with it," said Morgan. "If it wasn't for us darned kids." She kept a straight face for a moment before she burst out laughing.

Tiffany rolled her eyes. Morgan had been amusing herself ever since she tried to hit on Aaron. "Let's talk about the most important thing from today – are you going to tell Luke that Aaron rejected your affections?"

"Oh man," Morgan said with a groan. "Yeah – I have to come clean. And he'll know that I can't leave him because I simply can't get anyone else to date me."

Jade reached forward to pat her on the shoulder. "Aw, come on Morgan. You know that's not true. You will never leave him because you love him and you're crazy about him."

Morgan sighed. "This is true."

Tiffany smiled but said nothing. She couldn't even crack a joke about that. Both Jade and Morgan had wonderful boyfriends. She was happy for them. And if she was honest with herself, she now knew that she wanted that, too.

As tempted as she was to send Sidney a message with an update, she resisted. She didn't want to leave a digital trail linking them back to the hacking.

She'd just have to wait until Jade's journalist friend got this into the news. Maybe then, they could have another conversation.

Chapter 25

There was no word from Tiffany for the rest of the week, and by Friday, Sidney realized that he probably wouldn't hear from her again. Eric debated reaching out to Jade, but ultimately decided that Sidney was right and that it was probably time to let the project go.

The only thing lingering in Sidney's mind was the look on Tiffany's face when he brought up Steve. She looked completely puzzled – at first, he wondered if she even knew who Steve was. He doubted himself, but later decided that she was likely just surprised that he knew about Steve's bid.

Sidney tried not to think about any of it; the Clifton sisters were allowed to take their business wherever they wanted. They never signed a contract and had no duty to Burke Development. It was a sad way for things to turn out, but that was life.

On Friday afternoon, Sidney had a meeting with Uncle Dan to discuss progress. Eric wouldn't be there; he was busy talking to a potential client for a different job a few miles south of Seattle.

Sidney walked into Dan's office and shook his hand.

"So I hear you finally convinced Eric to go another direction?"

Sidney nodded. "I did. It was no easy task, but hopefully we can find an acceptable project to start with."

Dan let out a sigh. "Have a seat Sidney. Can I get you something to drink?"

"No, thank you. I'm all right." He got the distinct feeling that he was about to get a talking-to. He wasn't surprised; he'd been warning Eric about this for weeks. They couldn't keep dragging their feet and expect Dan to just let them get away without making any progress.

"I've been meaning to talk to you."

"Look, Uncle Dan," Sidney said, putting his hands up. "I know that we've been off to a rocky start. We're still in a phase of adjusting between expectations and reality, but now – "

Dan waved a hand. "I didn't bring you in here to berate you, Sid."

He sat back. "Oh."

"I wanted to talk to you about your future. You know how much it means to me that you're helping Eric. He's always needed someone to help him with – you know, to help guide his enthusiasm."

Sidney nodded. "Right, and I think we make a good team."

"And you do. You've given a lot to Eric, and he's come far. You both have. But I think he's old enough to stand on his own two feet. The person I'm worried about is you."

"Me?" Sidney felt like he'd walked into a wall. "I didn't realize that I was causing issues, I've always wanted to – "

"No, no – you never cause problems Sidney. You're hard-working, dedicated, and smart. You're business smart – not everybody has that. You know, I don't say this enough, but I'm proud of you."

Well this conversation wasn't going anywhere he'd expected. "Thanks Uncle Dan. That means a lot coming from you."

"But what I mean is – I don't want you to be stuck in Eric's shadow. Or babysitting him. Not that he needs a babysitter – don't tell him I said that."

Sidney shook his head. "I won't."

"But I feel like he's really hitting his stride – even if it's taking him a bit of time. So now I'm thinking about you – what do you want, Sidney? Where do you want to go?"

Sidney looked down, then back up at his uncle. "I...plan to keep working with Eric."

"No, no – I mean, what would you want to do if you weren't pulling Eric along?"

"You mean – instead of working with him?"

Dan nodded. "Yeah. If you were working with *your* best interest in mind – not just helping Eric achieve his dreams, but thinking about your own. What would you do?"

Sidney sat back in his chair. He always had a plan – he always stayed a few steps ahead. Recently, all of his plans revolved around Eric. He thought they'd be working together for years.

Sure, maybe one day he'd take off on his own. But there was always such a backlog of things to get done, so many tasks and fires to put out – he'd never thought of his future like this. He wasn't used to thinking in terms of his own best interest. That was something he assumed he'd think about once everyone else was settled. When – or rather, if – that day ever came.

"I'm...not sure."

"And I'm not saying that you can't keep working with Eric. But I want you to think about it and decide – is that really what you want?"

Sidney sat for a moment. He felt foolish that he hadn't considered this before, but why would he have? "I want to repay you for everything you've done for me. And..."

"I understand that, but son – you don't have to repay me for anything. You've earned your place. I'm betting that you've built up a substantial savings. And you're free to take that and build your own life. Heck – I'll be your first investor!"

"That's..." Sidney laughed. "That's definitely something to think about then."

Dan clapped his hands together. "Good! I don't want you to be sixty years old and look back on your life with regret."

Sidney nodded. He didn't want that either. He didn't think he was headed in that direction, but then again...

"All right, how about you show me what Eric's getting himself into?"

Sidney smiled. "Sure, I've got some of the plans right here."

The rest of their meeting went about as expected, as Sidney showed Dan the potential projects that they could end up working on.

On his way home from work that evening, Sidney called Eric to give him the good news that the meeting went well. Eric also said that one of the projects looked promising and that he was starting to get excited about some ideas.

When he got home, Sidney microwaved dinner and got back on his computer to catch up on emails. He was surprised to see an email from the Milky Way Star Awards. They'd sent along a thank you to their sponsors with a link containing photographs taken from that evening.

He knew that he shouldn't do it, but he clicked and started looking through the pictures. He was at least able to admit to himself what he was looking for – he hoped to see pictures of Tiffany from that night. From what he remembered, she looked quite stunning. Of course he hadn't noticed how beautiful she looked until he watched her walk into that club and retrieve Rachel; just before she made him aware that she'd overheard him insulting her...

Maybe this whole thing was just her getting back at him? She'd done a good job earning his trust, maybe it was all a ploy?

Sidney clicked through the pictures and was not disappointed. There were a handful of pictures of Tiffany – a few where she was in the background, and some where she'd posed with Jade. He lingered on them for perhaps too long, studying her smile and her big, bright eyes.

He then clicked through the rest of the pictures to see if there were any more of her. But instead of seeing more pictures from Tiffany, he came across a slew of pictures where Rachel looked quite friendly with a young looking guy that he didn't recognize.

Sidney had no memory of talking to these people – who were they? He zoomed in and saw the name tag on the guy – Aaron Corden.

Hm. That name didn't seem familiar. Sidney googled him and found out that he worked at the state parks department. That didn't seem too odd, then.

The guy had a ton of pictures online; he was definitely more active than the average parks employee. Sidney laughed to himself – Aaron seemed like quite the Casanova. No wonder Rachel ended up talking to him.

And perhaps maybe, just maybe, she'd learned something useful about the parks department? It was worth checking, and he was overdue to chat with her. He picked up his phone and called her.

Surprisingly, she answered. "Hello?"

"Hey Rachel, it's me. How're you doing?"

"Fine. How are you."

"I'm good. I had a question for you – I got some pictures from the Milky Way Star Awards and saw that you made a new friend. Aaron Corden?"

Rachel groaned. "Tiffany promised that she wouldn't tell."

"What? Tiffany knows him too?"

"Oh shoot." Silence for a beat. "Uh, no."

"Rachel. What did Tiffany promise not to tell me?"

She let out a sigh. "If I tell you, do you *promise* not to get mad at me?"

How could he promise something like that? It was impossible. "Rachel..."

"You have to promise! Nothing bad happened – not really."

He could feel the tension in his shoulders building. He was already getting angry, but he told himself he couldn't yell. That didn't seem to work with her at all. "Fine. I promise."

"I talked to him at the Milky Way Awards, and I thought he was, you know...nice. And he was a parks guy, so I thought I was, like, going to learn something useful."

"Okay. And did you?"

"Uh, sort of. And then he invited me to a fundraiser on Orcas Island, and I *knew* that you'd get mad and tell me I couldn't go, so...I didn't tell you about it."

Sidney let out a sigh. "Rachel, that's really far for you to go with someone that you don't know."

"I know, and I learned my lesson. He got weird after we got there and he kicked me out."

"What do you mean he got weird? Did he – "

"No, nothing like that. He just kind of told me I had to leave, and then left me outside."

Sidney gritted his teeth. A Casanova indeed. "That's ridiculous. How could he invite you and then leave you?"

She started talking quickly. "I know, but I couldn't tell you, so I called Tiffany and she came to pick me up. She said that I should tell you what happened, but I was afraid that you would yell at me. But nothing bad happened!"

"Wait a second," he said. "*Tiffany* picked you up?"

"Yeah. I don't have my car, *because if you remember* you took it away, so I got a ride from him on the way up, but then I was stuck there."

Sidney rubbed his face in his hands. What an ordeal.

"Hello? Are you still there?" Rachel asked.

"Yeah I'm just...processing this."

"And you can't get mad at Tiffany either! She thought that you might already know because you started ignoring her. And I was going to come clean eventually, I just thought that...I don't know, you just get so mad at me all of the time."

"I'm sorry Rachel, I don't mean to get mad at you. Believe it or not, I'm trying to help you."

"Yeah, I know."

He cleared his throat. "I'm glad that nothing bad happened to you."

"Me too, and I *promise* I won't do anything like that again."

Well, he didn't fully believe that. But at least she was talking to him, which was an improvement. "Good. When was it – this fundraiser?"

"Last week. On Friday."

Sidney covered his eyes with his hand. Of course.

Tiffany hadn't been meeting with Steve, betraying his trust – she hadn't betrayed him at all. In fact, she'd done him a huge favor! And he pushed her away. "Well...I'm glad you're safe. And I think that I owe Tiffany an apology."

"You're *still* not talking to her?"

And now even Rachel knew what an idiot he'd been. Great. He cleared his throat. "It's complicated."

"Oh...I'm sorry. I hope I didn't mess things up. I really like her. I mean, she kind of yelled at me when she was driving me home, but she was funny about it. She seems really nice."

"Yeah. Okay – well, I'll let you get back to your evening. And you're still coming to the office next week?"

"Yes! I'll see you on Monday."

"See you on Monday."

Sidney hung up the phone and sat back. This had been quite an eventful day. Not only did Uncle Dan point out that he'd completely forgotten to stop and think of his own goals, but he also discovered that Rachel was too scared of him to ask for help when she needed it. *And,* on top of everything, he'd been an absolute fool with Tiffany.

Now what?

Chapter 26

Around noon on Saturday, Margie was deep in thought, working away inside the barn, when she heard the back door fly open.

"Mom!" Jade yelled. "The story's out!"

Margie pushed a chair into place. "What story?"

"About the parks department funding!"

Margie frowned. Jade had been very mysterious when she discussed the origin of this. "Does that mean you'll finally tell me what you've been up to?"

Jade nodded. "Yes, now I can tell you everything. But look – read it!"

Margie accepted Jade's phone and squinted at the screen. "Honey, the text is too small for me to read without my glasses – can't you just tell me?"

"We'd better go inside and make some tea," Tiffany said as she joined them inside the barn. "I want you to be sitting down when you hear this."

"Oh boy," Margie said. "I hope that none of you are in any trouble!"

"No trouble at all!" Jade said. "It's all good news, I promise."

They went back to the house and Margie put on a kettle for tea. Morgan was already inside, laying out some cookies.

"Oh my, this is *quite* an event," Margie commented. "I feel like you three are trying to sell me something."

Jade laughed. "I just want you to keep an open mind."

The suspense was too much – Margie wished that the water would boil faster. She knew it would be good news, though – she hadn't seen Jade smile so much in weeks. When she finally got to take a seat, the girls sat across from her at the table as Jade read the article aloud.

Margie was shocked at what she heard. Jade's reporter friend, Marnie, detailed the scandalous story of the parks department's missing funding.

An employee, Aaron, used his position as an associate director in the department to funnel money to various fake contractors and shell companies. He would pretend to hire companies to add onto or maintain the parks, but he was really just using the money to enrich himself and his friends. He started to grow too bold, though, and took millions of dollars from the budget. That amount of money didn't go unnoticed.

"This is unbelievable!" said Margie. "They found all of this out with his emails?"

Jade nodded. "That's where it started. From there, Marnie worked with the FBI to uncover more details. It seems like the FBI was already suspicious and on the case – the emails just helped them piece it all together."

"Are they going to be able to get the money back?" asked Margie.

"Some of it," said Tiffany. "They froze all of the accounts, so that, at least, is good."

"Didn't you say that some of the money was going to political groups?" Margie asked.

"Now that's kind of tricky..." said Jade. "Apparently Marnie wasn't able to mention any of that in her story. She said she didn't have enough to point a finger at the senator involved. Not even the FBI wanted to tackle that – not yet, at least."

Margie set her tea down. "Why do I get the feeling that you three were involved?"

Morgan smiled broadly. "Because, Margie, we took a page out of *your* book and decided to do some of our own investigating."

She looked between the three of them. Tiffany was sitting calmly, Jade was avoiding eye contact, and Morgan was beaming. "And should I expect FBI agents to descend upon the house at any moment?"

Jade looked up. "No, nothing like that. We actually followed Tiffany's hunch and..."

"Jade stole the emails," Morgan blurted out. "It was awesome. Tiffany drove the getaway car, and I distracted Aaron with my newly discovered acting skills."

Margie put her hands up. "Hang on – what? Jade, did you really *steal* something?"

"Steal," Morgan said, clearing her throat and putting on her best Luke accent, "is such an *ugly* word."

Margie clutched her hands together. "I don't know if I want to hear this story."

Jade finished chewing a cookie before calmly explaining what had happened – it started with Tiffany rescuing Rachel, then Jeff's suggestion that they go looking for fraud, and finally, the successful attempt to get evidence to Marnie.

When she was done, Jade stared with a serious and pale face. "Are you mad at us, Mom?"

"Mad?" Margie sat back and crossed her arms. "No, I'm not mad. Though you did put yourselves in danger! And you didn't even include me!"

The three of them burst into laughter; Margie found herself laughing, too. It was one thing for the girls to get into trouble – but another thing entirely to hide it from her!

"Let's be honest Margie," Morgan leaned forward. "Would you really have *wanted* to be involved in that?"

She crossed her arms. "Maybe!"

"And would you have tried to talk us out of it?" asked Tiffany.

"Of course!"

Jade laughed and reached across the table to grab Margie's hand. "Luckily, the only person who knows what we did is Marnie, and she won't tell anyone. Besides – she said that the FBI didn't even ask how she got the emails. They were more interested in figuring out where all of the money was going."

"Well that's a relief," said Margie. "Honestly, I don't know where you girls get these ideas."

Tiffany laughed. "Right Mom – where can we *possibly* have learned to take matters into our own hands?"

Margie couldn't keep her face stern any longer – she laughed too. "Fair enough. I'm glad you at least had each other. What does this all mean, though? For the parks department?"

"Well, it's still being sorted out," said Jade. "But it seems like they've been able to recover several million dollars already. There's a chance that my grant might still be funded."

"That's wonderful news!" Margie said, clapping her hands together.

Jade nodded. "It is. It also means that the department isn't bankrupt."

"So," Tiffany added, "we stopped a sleazebag from ruining our beautiful state parks!"

Morgan turned to her. "Since when do you care so much about the parks? Have you even been outside since you moved here?"

Tiffany shrugged. "It's not so much about liking parks as it is about disliking sleazebags."

"Spoken like a true businesswoman who left the finance world in disgust," Morgan said with a smile.

As much as Margie didn't like the girls putting themselves into a situation like that, she was proud of them. They saw a wrong in the world and took steps to correct it.

The most surprising part of all was that Tiffany had *actually* spoken to her father. Margie thought she'd never forgive or speak to him again, but apparently, she'd gotten so desperate to figure out the fraud that she gave in.

Margie herself had felt an enormous sense of relief when she stopped covering up for Jeff's mistakes. She was angry for a lot of the things he had done, sure, but she was able to let a lot of that anger go and move on with her life.

But Tiffany's anger had simmered for so long. She refused to talk about any of it, and Margie felt helpless to relieve her of the feelings that grew into an ugly hatred. Perhaps Tiffany would never have a good relationship with her father, but at least now she seemed more at peace.

Here was Tiffany now, laughing and scheming with her sisters. Her walls were down, and Margie hoped that they would stay that way. Finally, it seemed, Tiffany had learned that she couldn't do everything on her own – and that she didn't need to.

Margie excused herself to the kitchen so that she could throw something together for lunch. Tiffany followed her.

"I'm proud of you sweetie," Margie said, giving her a hug. "Are you hungry? I'm going to make something."

"Thanks Mom. And actually...I may be going out for lunch."

"Oh? With who?"

"Sidney. He just called me."

Margie stopped what she was doing. "I thought that he was refusing to talk to you?"

"I thought so too. But he said that he wanted to meet up."

"Perhaps he heard about the news story?"

Tiffany shook her head. "That's what I thought at first, but I actually surprised him when I told him about it."

"Oh," Margie said. She studied her daughter for a moment – her arms were crossed and her eyes were focused on a spot far away. "So are you going to meet with him?"

"Well, I don't want to miss lunch if you're doing something, I can just tell him – "

"No please, don't skip on my behalf."

Tiffany said nothing.

It was no mystery to Margie what was going on with her daughter, even if Tiffany refused to discuss it. She was excellent at avoiding the topic, too, but Margie wasn't a fool.

Finally, Margie spoke again. "You like this guy, don't you?"

Tiffany uncrossed her arms. "I do, but..."

"But what?"

She sighed. "He's coming up here, and he wants to *talk*."

Margie nodded. "And this is bad because...?"

"Because I don't know what to say to him. I mean, maybe he finally knows about Rachel and I can apologize about that but...what else am I going to say? I don't know what he thinks about me, I don't know how he feels..."

"Of course you can't know those things – not without taking a risk." Margie smiled. "My darling. You know that falling in love is reserved for the brave, right?"

Tiffany was quiet for a moment. "Courage *is* an important value."

Margie didn't know what she meant by that, but she agreed with the sentiment. "Yes. And it's much easier to be cynical, and to make excuses, and to never let anyone in."

"That's very true," said Tiffany with a half smile. "I've done it for years."

Margie laughed. "That's not true! Though love is a risk that we all have to take, or else risk our hearts withering away."

"Isn't that a little dramatic?" Tiffany said, finally breaking into a full smile.

Margie loved Tiffany's smile – and loved that she was seeing it more often these days. "Maybe. Maybe not. It's up to you to decide who is worth risking your heart over. And it's up to you to decide to be brave."

Tiffany gave her mom a kiss on the cheek. "Thanks Mom. Then I guess...I'll be back later?"

"Good. Have a nice time!"

Chapter 27

After he parked his car on the ferry, Sidney found a comfortable window seat and pulled out his phone. He found the article that Tiffany had told him about when he'd called and quickly read through it.

Once he reached the end, he read it again. It was astonishing. For every question that it answered, though, two more popped into his mind. Was Rachel involved in this? Where did those emails come from? And how did the FBI figure this out so quickly? Most of all, why did he get the distinct feeling that Tiffany was somehow involved?

When he finally was able to leave the ferry, he drove straight to the deli where Tiffany agreed to meet him. She was already inside when he walked in. As usual, she'd beat him to it.

"Hi Tiffany," he said when they locked eyes.

She smiled. "Sidney, good to see you. I'm glad that you could make it."

He took a seat across from her. "I actually left quite early this morning but there was an accident, and we were in standstill traffic for almost two hours."

"Oh, that's unpleasant. Well – what brings you here?"

He cleared his throat. "I came here to see you. First off, to apologize."

She raised her eyebrows. "Oh."

He continued. "I've made a lot of mistakes in my life, not the least of which was doubting you. I'm truly sorry about the way I've been acting and how I treated you when you visited my office this week. I was more than rude – I was an idiot."

Tiffany smiled. "I seem to have that effect on men."

"Is that so?"

"Yeah. Well – people sometimes think that I'm much more nefarious than I actually am." She laughed. "I think it's my face."

He quite liked her face, but he couldn't tell her that now. "Well, whatever the case, I'm sorry. There's no excuse for it. I was led to believe that you canceled our plans because you were working with an acquaintance of ours – Steve Wilmington."

Tiffany nodded. "I figured that out eventually. Jade got his bid and was so bewildered by him that she didn't even mention it to me. I had no idea."

"I realize that now. But it was only after Rachel told me about her mishap on Orcas Island that I understood what actually happened. And I realized what a jerk I've been."

Tiffany sat there, hands folded on the table, watching him with those big eyes. She was smiling; a sort of half smile, and her stare was unbroken.

He kept talking. "I have to thank you, *really* thank you, for helping Rachel."

"You're welcome. She's a great girl. She's just young and... angry. I get it," Tiffany said with a laugh. "I mean, I'm thirty years old and I just realized that anger has been driving me for most of my life."

Sidney smiled. "And now?"

"And now..." She drummed her fingers on the table. "I'm trying to make decisions about my life more consciously. I'm glad you're here, actually."

"Oh?"

"I wanted to tell you a bit about that article."

He cleared his throat. "Of course. I read it on the ferry – it's unbelievable. I mean, it's awful what Aaron did, but wonderful that he's been caught."

Tiffany looked around before focusing her eyes back on him. "There's more to that story. Can I trust you not to tell anyone?"

Sidney thought he had no right to her trust, but felt honored that she would even consider him. "Absolutely."

"It all started because of Rachel, actually. She said that Aaron kicked her out of that fundraiser when he got into a spat with a senator – Senator Kathy Shields. Do you know her?"

Sidney frowned. "I don't believe so."

"Well, since we weren't working together, I had to figure this out on my own. Unfortunately, I had to talk to my dad, who gave me some ideas. And then...we had to get creative."

Sidney narrowed his eyes. "What exactly does that mean?"

Tiffany looked over her shoulder again. There was no one anywhere near them. "Actually – let's get our lunch to go?"

They went to the counter and both picked out some ready-made sandwiches. Sidney had no idea what he was in for, but he didn't care. He could listen to her talk all day. He loved the mischief in her eyes and the way that she used her hands so much when she spoke.

Once they had their food, they walked down the street until they reached a secluded bench overlooking the water. There, Tiffany told him the remarkable story of how she and her sisters broke into Aaron's computer and stole the emails that implicated him in the fraud.

Sidney sat stunned, unsure how to respond. She was even more remarkable than he realized.

And he'd messed it all up.

She took a bite of her sandwich. "Now you know the full story. So basically, the next time you get mad and want to get back at me, you can just turn me in to the police."

Sidney laughed. "I would never do that. But what does this mean for Jade's park?"

"We're hoping that she'll be able to get the money that she was promised in the grant. It might take some time to work out, though – the FBI needs to free up the funds. But we're hopeful."

"I understand if you no longer want to do business with me, but please don't take any of that out on Eric. He's blameless in this." Sidney sighed. "I realize that I'm a liability. So you won't have to work with me anymore – you can work directly with Eric. I believe he'll promote one of his employees to take over my responsibilities, too."

"Where are you going?" Tiffany asked, eyebrows furrowed.

"I don't know yet. I'm thinking that I need to start something for myself. And I need to...confront some uncomfortable truths about myself."

"But why?" Tiffany's hand darted over to rest on top of his. "Why do you have to leave?"

Sidney felt like he lost his breath for a moment. Her touch was so soft but unexpected, he felt a chill run down his back. He had to take a moment to respond appropriately. "I find that it's impossible for me to be impartial to you, Tiffany. And I don't want to hold you back."

"Why would you need to stay impartial?"

He was mesmerized by her stare and her gentle touch. He studied her for a moment before taking her hand into his. "Because I think you're brilliant, and beautiful, and fascinating. And apparently, I'm too much of a brute to behave professionally and not jump to conclusions about your intentions."

Tiffany took her other hand and delicately brushed away a crop of hair that the wind blew onto his forehead. "Which intentions do you mean, exactly?"

He couldn't bear it any longer – he felt that she would soon turn them into a puddle. He pulled away so that she was no longer touching his face.

"I'm never quite sure if you're toying with me, Tiffany."

She let out a sigh. "Sidney Burke, I've tried my hardest to always be nice to you, to try to impress you, and let's be honest, show up before you to all of our meetings – and apparently, all of my attempts to flirt with you have failed. I'm an even worse flirt than Morgan. But let me be clear – I have never *once* tried to toy with you."

So he hadn't imagined it; she'd felt it too. Even though he'd started off their relationship by insulting her, she didn't hold it against him. Even though he jumped to conclusions and assumed the worst about her, she didn't give up on proving him wrong.

And he was wrong at every turn – because Tiffany *was* as wonderful as she seemed. She was someone that he should have counted on, but instead, he let his own insecurities get in the way.

He was still gazing into her eyes when she leaned in, touching her forehead to his. They smiled at each other for a moment before he couldn't take it anymore – he drew her in and kissed her fiercely.

She relaxed her weight against him, wrapping one arm behind his neck. After a moment, Sidney broke their embrace, pulling away slightly to study her face again. He could feel the goosebumps rippling down his back as she gently ran her fingers through his hair.

"I've been waiting a very long time to do that," he said.

"I'm glad that we could finally make it happen," she replied, closing her eyes before leaning in to delicately kiss him on the cheek.

"So if you had a choice about me leaving, you'd say – "

"That you'd better not leave me high and dry with this nightmare of a park."

He smiled and leaned forward to kiss her again. "If you insist."

Chapter 28

It took a few months, but Tiffany felt good about where she was leaving Jade's park project.

"It's not going to be the same without you," Morgan said with an airy sigh. "What if I need you to drive another getaway car for me?"

Tiffany was prepared for all of this questioning. "Well, I'm sure that my mom will be more than happy to help. She's now insisting that she would've been an asset to us."

"I can't believe you're leaving," Jade said, her bottom lip jutting out to an almost pout.

"Don't worry sis – I won't be *that* far. And Olympia isn't that bad of a drive."

"It's not far at all if Sidney will fly you over," Morgan said with a smile.

"I told you that he doesn't have access to that now that he's starting his own company."

Morgan shrugged. "I'm betting that Eric will be more than willing to share his helicopter. And his plane. And his boat. They're still family!"

"Be that as it may," Tiffany said as she taped up a box containing books and items from her desk, "driving suits us both just fine."

Tiffany caught sight of Jade, still standing there cross-armed and looking sad. Tiffany turned toward her. "I've loved my time here with you guys, I *really* have. You both taught me so much. But...I need to spread my wings and fly!"

Jade laughed at her cheesy joke. "I know. I just wish it could last forever."

"Who knows," Tiffany said with a shrug. "If my and Sidney's business is successful, maybe we'll buy ourselves a little cabin on San Juan Island and spend weekends here."

Jade's eyes brightened. "Oh, do you mean it?"

"Of course!"

"What do you mean *we*?" Morgan said. "Are you and Sidney already planning everything as a couple?"

"Well, no." Tiffany nodded. "But we talk about our future a lot."

Morgan sighed. "I guess he is almost forty years old. And a bit more mature than Luke."

"Yeah, you could say that." Tiffany smiled. "But he's not *almost* forty! He's thirty-six. Soon to be thirty-seven..."

"That rounds to forty," Morgan countered.

Sidney was certainly more serious than Luke was. He wasted no time in figuring out what he wanted to do after making up his mind to move on from Burke Development.

And he made no secret that he wanted Tiffany by his side – both in love and in business.

Since they made up, they'd hardly spent more than a few days apart. Sidney was always popping in, whether by car, helicopter, or plane. He even took everyone out on the yacht one day and Tiffany was so delighted to see him with her family. He fit in with Matthew and Luke, and even Chief took a liking to him.

Her mom, of course, showered him with attention and praise, which he graciously accepted, once he got past his embarrassment.

He was honestly better than anything she could have dreamed up. He was endlessly kind, and she could spend hours talking to him – or staring at him. Her favorite was seeing his beautiful, dark features light up with a smile. It was much more common now, though he did still walk around many days with a scowl, deep in thought.

One night, after they'd been dating for about a month, he told her that he'd never known it was possible to be so happy.

"I think about you all of the time, and when I'm not with you, just the idea of you can brighten my day. Just knowing that you exist makes the world a worthwhile place," he'd said.

"That's exactly how I feel," Tiffany responded. "I'm half torn between being terrified that it's all going to come crashing down, and convinced that I'm losing my mind."

"I'm with you on that," he said. He took her hand and planted a kiss on it. "But I've never been so happy to lose my mind."

"Uh Tiffany? Are you still with us?" asked Morgan.

Tiffany snapped back to the present. She'd never been one to daydream, so this was a new challenge for her. "Yeah – sorry."

"We'd better get going if you want to get to Sunday dinner on time," said Jade. "Are you ready?"

Tiffany nodded. "Yeah – I can finish packing up later."

They piled into Jade's car and headed over. Tiffany felt giddy during the drive – Sidney was coming to dinner and she couldn't wait to see him. She loved seeing him interact with her family and friends; when she doubted that he was real and that he was as charming as she remembered, she only needed to hear Luke making fun of him to assuage her fears.

Their plan for the future was a bit wild, so she was careful to ask the opinion of her mom, her sisters, and even Chief Hank. She knew she could trust them to tell her the truth.

Luckily, no one thought that she was being hasty and they all agreed that Sidney was a solid business partner. His plan was to start a new company that would develop and build community sites – not just parks, but anything that people needed, from senior centers, to recreation centers, to affordable apartments. He had his heart set on improving the communities that he touched, and Tiffany was delighted to go along for the ride.

Not that she was just "going along," though. He asked her to work with him to establish contacts, secure funding, and meet with clients and contractors. The only experience she had was working on Jade's park, but she'd loved the challenge. It didn't take much convincing.

He'd gotten himself an apartment in Olympia weeks ago, but hadn't wanted to move until Tiffany was able to move to her apartment, too. She was a bit old-fashioned and wanted to have her own place, though – even if it was only half a mile from his.

She had to have some boundaries, because she'd never been swept up in a romance like this before, and she was afraid that she was going to lose her head.

When they got to the house, she was disappointed to see that his car wasn't there. Perhaps he'd gotten caught up with work?

But as soon as she walked in, she spotted him, standing and laughing with the other guys, looking very handsome in his light blue button up shirt. She loved seeing him without a tie – he just *looked* more relaxed.

"You're here!" she said, giving him a kiss.

"You have me to thank for that," said Luke. "I picked up this jet setter at the airport on my way over. You'd think he could've landed his helicopter on top of the barn, but no! Apparently that's not how it works."

Sidney laughed. "It's not."

As everyone else was saying their hellos, Sidney leaned down and whispered in her ear, "I've missed you."

She laughed. "I saw you two days ago in Seattle."

"It's been two days too long."

She rolled her eyes at him and was about to turn her attention to say hello to her mom when she felt a tug on her elbow. She turned around to see Sidney down on one knee.

She gasped. "What's the matter?"

"I can't wait any longer to do this," he said. "I bought this ring a month after we started dating."

He popped open the red velvet box, revealing a gorgeous ring with an intricate, decadent setting.

Tiffany gaped at him, speechless. The entire room was silent now.

"I didn't know that I was waiting my entire life to meet you, but now I need to make up for lost time. You're like a dream to me and I'm afraid I'll wake up at any moment. Will you marry me?"

Tiffany blinked several times, finding herself unable to speak.

"For goodness sake, if you don't marry him I will!" said Luke.

"Yes," Tiffany finally said. "A hundred times, yes!"

A smile spread across Sidney's face; he placed the ring on her finger before standing up and kissing her. The room erupted in cheers and laughter.

"Oh good!" her mom said. "I was hoping that you'd say yes."

"You knew?" Tiffany said, incredulous.

"Of course," she said with a shrug. "Sidney asked for my permission."

Now that made Tiffany laugh – as though her mother would ever refuse him. "And I'm guessing you said yes?"

A smile spread across her mom's face. "Of course! Hang on a second."

She darted into the kitchen and came back out carrying a cake. Tiffany leaned over to see what it said – "It's about time!"

They both burst into laughter.

"I thought you would like that," she said with a smile.

"That's a good one, Mom," Tiffany said. She couldn't stop smiling. She looked up at Sidney. How had he managed to pull this off without her knowing?

She'd have to get the details later. Now Jade and Morgan were fussing over the ring, and Luke was putting in a request to have cake before dinner.

Though she'd gotten off to a bumpy start, it seemed like thirty was a good year for her after all. She gave Sidney another kiss before turning to cut the cake.

Epilogue

After Connor got back from his five day backpacking trip in the mountains, he decided that he would unpack his bag right away. In the past, there were times when he threw his backpack on the floor and spent the week (or longer) avoiding it.

But this time, he was going to be responsible. He was about halfway through it when he came across his cell phone.

Oh right – it had run out of charge days ago. His mom had bought him a solar-powered phone charger, but unfortunately, on the first day of camping, it fell into a creek and it never worked again.

Oh well! He liked being able to disconnect from his phone. That was one of his favorite things about going out into nature – whether he was camping, kayaking, or even when he was doing his duty as a tour guide. It was even better when he could get the people who he took out on tours to disconnect, too.

But it was time to come back to reality, if only for a while. He picked up the phone and plugged it in to charge. He knew he'd have a bunch of emails to sort through about his next seasonal job. He'd applied to a few places for the summer – a ranch in Colorado, a kayaking company in Jackson Hole and a bike tour place in Montana.

A few of his friends were moving to Mexico to become scuba instructors and tried to convince him to tag along. Years ago, he would've jumped at the opportunity; but now, he was on his fourth year of jumping from one seasonal gig to another. It wasn't as exciting as it once was and he was having a hard time picking where to go next.

He finished unpacking his bag and was going to make himself something to eat when he walked by his phone and noticed that he had a slew of missed phone calls and text messages.

A bunch of them were from his sisters, mainly Tiffany. When she lived in Chicago, she hardly texted him at all. But ever since she moved out to Washington, she was always checking in on him and sending pictures of Mom and the house.

It was kind of an odd change in Tiffany, but he liked it. The only thing that he didn't like was that now he was the *only* member of the family living far away; he really felt left out sometimes.

With an apple in one hand, and his phone in the other, he gave Tiffany a call back.

"Thank goodness you're okay!" Tiffany said as soon as she answered.

He laughed. "Sorry sis. I went camping and my phone died. Then I broke the solar charger. And actually, I probably didn't have service anyway..."

"But you're fine?"

"Yeah I'm fine, don't worry so much."

"Well Mom isn't okay. She had an accident."

His heart dropped into his stomach. "What? What happened?"

"Well, she's okay now – mostly. She was riding mopeds with Chief. They rented them. Anyway – they were just riding around the island when these people in a moving van sideswiped them."

"Oh my gosh."

"Chief broke his leg. Mom broke her elbow, her hip, and a couple of ribs."

Connor took a seat. This was not what he'd expected to hear when he called back. "I can't believe this. Are they going to be okay?"

"Yeah, they will. Mom especially has a few weeks ahead of her that are going to be tough."

"That's terrible."

Tiffany sighed. "And *then* I started getting really worried about you because you weren't answering your phone! You can't just leave the face of the earth like that."

Connor cleared his throat. "I know. I'm really sorry. When did this happen?"

"On Sunday."

He counted back in his head. "Wait, this was *four* days ago?"

"Yeah little bro! We couldn't reach you. But whatever, I'm glad I finally got a hold of you."

"Yeah, me too. I'm going to book a flight right now – I'll be there soon. I'll let you know when I can be there, okay?"

"Okay, sounds good."

"Are you with Mom now? Can I talk to her?"

"No, I'm at the house."

Connor stood up to find his laptop. "Where's Mom?"

"She's at the hospital – in Bellingham."

Connor closed his eyes. How could he have missed this? What if something worse had happened? "I'm going to give her a call, thanks Tiffany."

"Sure."

He called his mom's cell phone but she didn't answer. Maybe she was sleeping? He started googling the injuries that she had. It sounded pretty serious – the broken elbow especially seemed like it would take a long time to heal. And the broken ribs too! He had no idea how serious broken ribs were.

Connor paced back and forth in his room. He could hear his roommates loudly carrying on and laughing – it sounded like they were watching a movie.

Connor tried calling his mom again, but there was still no answer. He started looking at flights to Seattle and had one picked out. When should he book his trip back, though? He couldn't decide, and something just felt off. He couldn't put his finger on it.

That night, he had trouble sleeping. He kept running through the fact that his mom could have died and he was hundreds of miles away and completely unreachable. What kind of a son was he? How could anyone in the family count on him if that's how hard it was to reach him in an emergency?

The next morning, his mom finally called him back. "Hi honey! So good to hear from you!"

"Hey Mom, I am so, so sorry that I've been out of touch. I went backpacking with the guys and – "

"Oh it's okay! Don't worry, I'm fine. I just had a little fall." She chuckled. "And so did Hank. But we're on the mend. I had a couple of surgeries and now I just need to recover."

Connor winced. A *couple* of surgeries? What a nightmare. "Can you walk? I mean – how long are you going to be in the hospital?"

"Oh, not long I'm sure. And no, I can't really walk...they want to send me to a rehab facility for a bit. And then...then I'm not sure. It's going to be hard getting around, and Hank also has a broken leg, so he's not of much use either! But I'm sure that we'll figure it out. Jade and Morgan aren't too far."

Connor's heart sank. He felt like the scum of the earth. Was he really going to let his sisters take full responsibility for their injured mother? While he hiked around the mountains and kayaked?

No.

"Mom, I'm coming back."

"I would love to see you!"

"No – I mean, I'm moving back. I'm going to be there for whenever you get home, and help you with everything that you need."

"Oh honey, that's not necessary. I know you're very happy out in Colorado and – "

"No Mom, I'm serious. I've had enough time out here. How long will it be before you're home?"

"Oh, I don't know. They said I'll be here another week or so. Then probably about two weeks at the rehab facility..."

Ouch. Those were some serious injuries. "And I bet that you can't go home unless there's someone there to help you?"

"Don't worry, sweetheart! I'm sure I'll figure it out."

"Mom – I'll be there in two weeks to get everything ready. Okay? I'm so sorry. And I'm so glad that you're okay. I love you."

She let out a little huff. "I love you too sweetie."

"Talk to you soon."

Connor felt a weight lift off of his shoulders. No wonder he was having a hard time picking his job for the next season – he'd overstayed his time as a nomad.

Sure, it'd been a lot of fun and he'd gotten to meet a lot of great people. But how long was he going to go on like that?

His family needed him – his mom needed him.

It was time to grow up. And it was time to join the rest of the Clifton clan on San Juan Island.

Introduction to *Saltwater Falls*

Lights, camera...romance!

Now that Connor is home on San Juan Island, he knows it's time to give up his carefree lifestyle and put down some roots. But then he meets a Hollywood-bound beauty and starts to question everything...

Teresa has only one goal. She will succeed as a location scout for her first big-time film. Falling for the distractingly handsome Connor was not on her agenda. *Oops...*

When disturbing secrets that could ruin the movie—and Teresa's career—come to light, will Connor do the right thing and risk losing the love of his life? And more importantly, if he does, will Teresa be able to open her heart enough to trust what he has to say?

Saltwater Falls, book 5 in the Westcott Bay series, is a sweet women's fiction story that features a hint of danger, a guaranteed happily ever after, and the kind of true love that can always be found on San Juan Island. Get your copy of *Saltwater Falls* today and get ready to do some serious binge reading!

Author's Note

Special thanks to Andy Howard, Esq., my dear friend and one of Pittsburgh's finest attorneys, who generously provided his legal opinion and expertise for Andrea's case.

Would you like to join my reader group?

Sign up for my reader newsletter and get a free copy of my novella Christmas at Saltwater Cove. You can sign up by visiting: https://bit.ly/XmasSWC

About the Author

Amelia Addler writes always sweet, always swoon-worthy romance stories and believes that everyone deserves their own happily ever after.

Her soulmate is a man who once spent five weeks driving her to work at 4AM after her car broke down (and he didn't complain, not even once). She is lucky enough to be married to that man and they live in Pittsburgh with their little yellow mutt. Visit her website at AmeliaAddler.com or drop her an email at amelia@AmeliaAddler.com.

Also by Amelia...

The Westcott Bay Series

Saltwater Cove

Saltwater Studios

Saltwater Secrets

Saltwater Crossing

Saltwater Falls

Saltwater Memories

Saltwater Promises

Christmas at Saltwater Cove

The Orcas Island Series

Sunset Cove

The Billionaire Date Series

Nurse's Date with a Billionaire

Doctor's Date with a Billionaire

Veterinarian's Date with a Billionaire

Made in the USA
Monee, IL
23 May 2023

34387138R00136